Highland Valentine

A Highland Secrets Story

highland valentine

a highland secrets story

by

c.a. szarek

Highland Valentine
C.A. Szarek

A Highland Secrets Story

Paper Dragon Publishing
North Richland Hills, TX

eBook ISBN: 978-1-941151-21-1
Print book ISBN: 978-1-941151-22-8

Published in the United States of America

First eBook Edition: February, 2017
First Print Edition: October, 2016

Second eBook Edition: August, 2023
Second Print Edition: August, 2023

Other Books by C.A. Szarek

<u>Highland Secrets Trilogy & Companions—Historical Fantasy Romance</u>

The Princess and The Laird (Highland Secrets Prequel)

The Tartan MP3 Player (Book One)

The Fae Ring (Book Two)

The Parchment Scroll (Book Three)

Highland Valentine (A Highland Secrets HEA Story)

Highlander's Portrait (A Highland Secrets Story)

<u>Highland Treasures—Historical Fantasy Romance</u>

Highland Oath (Book One)

Highland Essence (Book Two)

Highland Skies (Book Three)

<u>The King's Riders—Fantasy Romance</u>

Sword's Call (Book One)—*Also in Audio*

Love's Call (Book Two)—*Also in Audio*

Rogue's Call (Book Three)—*Also in Audio*

Fate's Call (A Novella from the World of the King's Riders)—*Also in Audio*

<u>**Crossing Forces — Romantic Suspense**</u>
Collision Force (Book One) — *Also in Audio*

Cole in Her Stocking (A Crossing Forces Christmas) — ***FREE read!***

Chance Collision (Book Two) — *Also in Audio*

Calculated Collision (Book Three) — *Also in Audio*

Collision Control (Book Four) — *Also in Audio*

Weekend Collision (A Crossing Forces HEA Story) — ***FREE read!***

Superior Collision (Book Five) — *Also in Audio*

Incendiary Collision (Book Six) — *Coming Soon!*

<u>**The Giovanni**</u>
King of Hearts (Book One) — *Also in Audio*

Queen of Diamonds (Book Two) — *Coming Soon!*

dedication

This one goes out to my fab editor, Fiona, who is as excited about my Highland stories as I am. Thanx for loving Jules and Hugh like I do!

chapter one

Jules folded her softest sleeping chemise and put it on top of the bundle. If she could manage a trunk, she would've, but a few dresses and what passed for underwear in 1676 would have to do.

She sniffled, refused to give in to her hovering tears. If she thought about the devastation rocking just below the surface, she'd crumble. Or worse—lose her nerve. She pushed it all away, concentrating on the task at hand.

I have to do what I have to do.

Like always.

Jules hadn't been able to get a bag, so she'd set her belongings at the center of a fresh bed sheet she'd had one of the servant girls bring her. Not that she'd ever be questioned, but she wanted to be as inconspicuous as possible. For Hugh's sake, if nothing else. Gossip ran rampant around this place.

She wrapped it up like a present and tied the bundle off.

The baby moved and her hand shot over the spot on the left side of her distended tummy, but she didn't rub there. It was as if her husband's child was protesting her plan.

Tears burned her eyes.

Jules shook her head and swiped at her cheeks. The room she'd shared with the big Highlander for just over a year blurred despite her resolve.

He'd lived alone in this room for many more years than she'd been with him, so the furniture was all masculine, oversized, and dark wood—except for the trunk at the end of their bed he'd carved and given her the day they'd been married.

That day—the happiest of her life—felt like a sad memory right now.

The work on the piece was intricate. Hugh had used his talent to the fullest. The border was made up of detailed swords, thistles, and swirls in a pattern. It almost looked as if he'd had modern day computer and engraving equipment for such a delicate design.

He'd put her name at the center, but the surname 'MacDonald' dominated next to it and shook her soul as she gazed down on what she couldn't take with her. Jules was his wife, the Lady of Armadale, but lately she didn't feel that.

She avoided looking at the bed they'd made love

in so many times. She could feel the warmth of the fire behind her and smell the fresh peat burning. This room had comforted her often since she'd traveled back in time to seventeenth century Scotland in search of her sister. Her surroundings were *him*, like nothing she'd ever wanted before, and now something she couldn't keep.

"Juliette?" His voice made her jump.

She crushed her eyes shut and took a fortifying breath. She was going to need any strength she could muster.

Jules whirled toward the man she loved.

The love of her life.

She made no effort to hide the clothes she'd packed—he'd know her intentions in moments, and to say he wasn't going to be happy about it was putting it mildly. Hugh always yelled and barked orders, so she had to be ready for it. Her insides wobbled—and this time it wasn't the baby she carried.

Their eyes locked and she hollered at herself to not get lost in his beautiful midnight orbs like she always did. She held on to the hurt from the past months with both hands. Talked herself out of second and third, fourth, maybe even the hundredth chance Jules had given him to stop smashing her hopes. Talking to him, or trying to, had gotten her nowhere.

The only thing Hugh MacDonald hadn't destroyed was her love for him, but at that moment, Jules wished she didn't love him.

Maybe she wouldn't be dying inside if she could hate him.

Her eyes trailed his tall form, broad shoulders, trim waist. His ebony hair was messy as usual, and in need of a good cut as it fell to his shoulders. His face was clean-shaven; his chiseled cheekbones and jaw lines begging for a touch even across their room.

Looking at his full mouth made Jules swallow, because she wanted to taste him. Kissing Hugh was out. He'd barely looked at her in months, let alone touched…kissed…held her. He hadn't made love to her since the night she'd told him she was pregnant.

Her husband usually wore trews, but today he was clad in a kilt of his clan's tartan pattern—what he would refer to as a plaid—and Jules shut down the zing of awareness that hit her.

His ivory tunic, or leine as they called them, wasn't tight, but the defined muscles of his chest were as beautiful as his rare smile. She couldn't see them, but she remembered every inch of his body. Even mad as hell at him, he was the hottest thing she'd ever seen.

Mad's not right.

She wasn't mad. She was…

"Juliette?" Hugh repeated.

Her name rolled over her in his thick brogue. It got her every time, as well as his refusal to call her by her nickname, even after a year of marriage. He always said her name was too beautiful to shorten.

Jules jolted. Cleared her throat. Tried to shut down

her draw to him. "I'm leaving, Hugh."

Silence fell, but she couldn't look away. To keep her hands busy, she lifted the bundle of her belongings and held it in front of her. It wasn't heavy, but it wasn't much.

Hugh's gaze fell to her tummy, but then he averted his eyes and shifted in his boots. Like evidence of their child on her body burned him.

Disappointment crashed down and she bit her bottom lip to keep it from trembling. Sucked back the urge to cry and swallowed again—this time against the lump in her throat.

"I dinnae understand," he said finally.

"Yes, you do. If you didn't, you wouldn't be looking at me like that." She cursed the shake in her words.

"Ye dinnae leave me." This was harder. More like her husband.

He wasn't *ordering* her to stay?

That wasn't Hugh-like. The man she loved was usually full of orders and commands where she was concerned. They argued about such things so much she'd accused him of loving to fight with her. Then again, they hadn't had a real tiff in months. As if Jules' pregnancy had shut down his personality.

"I—"

Hugh closed the distance between them, so she snapped her mouth shut, but he didn't reach for her like she wanted. Needed. Craved.

That might've changed her mind.

Another wave of sadness washed over her, and Jules now had a meteor in her throat. It was growing. Soon she wouldn't be able to speak.

She was two seconds from a total breakdown, but she couldn't—wouldn't—do that in front of him.

"Dinnae go." This was low, a plea more than anything else. Hugh's eyes implored, but again, Jules couldn't look at him.

Her *everything* hurt.

"I have to," she whispered, but it was a croak more than anything. Jules cleared her throat and studied her bundle. Her arms framed her stomach, pressing the fabric of her simple saffron gown to her body, and making her roundness prominent.

She'd never been fond of dresses, but as her baby grew, she'd had to give up corsets, leines and trews. Her husband never liked her in what he called '*lad's clothing*,' anyway.

"The bairn…"

"Is as much mine as yours," she forced out.

Hugh was silent for several moments, so she glanced up at him. His expression was unreadable, those dark eyes almost as emotionless as they were fathomless.

Wasn't that just like her man?

He shook his head, making his thick locks dance, and she wanted to drop her clothing and run her hands through them. Tame his hair, like she'd thought she'd tamed him. Jules hadn't at all. She'd always liked him wild and unbridled, but not broken, like he was before her.

"That dinnae be what I meant," he whispered.

Not what she'd expected him to say, but her husband, never a man of many words, didn't expand on his statement.

That just hurt more.

He wouldn't talk to her, no matter what she'd tried. Begging, pleading, questioning just made Hugh grumpy and he'd yell. Demanding didn't work, either. That would just make him bristle, then shut down.

"Claire is picking me up," Jules blurted.

His Adam's apple bobbed and his jaw set, but he didn't say anything. He didn't even wear the normal scowl he usually reserved for mention of anything MacLeod.

Her younger sister had come back in time before Jules, and had married Duncan MacLeod, the twin brother of the current Laird MacLeod. The clan, which lived on the other side of the Isle of Skye, had warred with Clan MacDonald for hundreds of years.

They'd been at peace since Hugh's father was the laird, but neither party was fond of each other.

For the sakes of Claire and Jules, they tried. Only because Hugh had saved her sister's son, as far as her brother-in-law was concerned.

She wrote to her sister weekly — if not more — and saw her often. Over the past few months, Claire had been the only reason she'd remained sane. Here at Armadale—the MacDonald stronghold—she had Hugh's aunt, Mab, but she'd not been completely honest with the older woman. Jules couldn't open up to her like she could to her sister.

"Ye will go ta Dunvegan?" Her husband's broad shoulders slumped.

He really isn't going to argue?

Order me to unpack and stay?

Defeat and agony hit her in waves, and Jules clutched the knot she'd made on the linen until her knuckles whitened and her fingertips ached. Her legs wobbled, but she locked her knees. She couldn't risk her baby with a fall.

She couldn't confirm his question aloud, but she didn't need to. Hugh had been correct, but it wasn't like she had anywhere else to go, anyway.

Jules inhaled again and swallowed for the hundredth time that morning. Squared her shoulders and forced one foot in front of the other.

Move. Walk past him. Just get out of here.

"I love ye, Juliette."

Jules almost lost it. Threw a hand to the doorframe when she hit the threshold so she wouldn't fall over but didn't break into a run like she wanted to. It was difficult enough to walk around, as pregnant as she was. Wouldn't be able to run if she tried.

She closed her eyes and ordered air in and out as normally as possible. Forbade herself from turning back to her husband or rushing into his arms.

Jules loved him, too. More than she'd ever thought possible, but she loved the life growing within her, as well. More than her own. More than her love for Hugh, possibly.

So, she had to leave.

"This isn't about love." She pushed words out because she couldn't deny loving her husband aloud. Nor would she hurt him like that, with a lie. Like he'd hurt her. Jules kept her back to him, reminding herself to be strong and just leave.

Two more steps and she'd be in the corridor. She'd follow it to the stairs that led down to the great hall, and then go out into the bailey, where her ride should be soon. In her last letter, Claire had said they'd leave Dunvegan at first light.

"Dinnae? What else then?" Hugh's voice cracked.

Tears scorched Jules' cheeks and she cursed them. She wiped her face and sucked back a sob. The baby moved and she tried to ignore it. Refused to focus on the fact she was taking her child from his or her father. "You know where I'll be."

It wasn't like he was going to come after her—*them*—if he was willing to let her go.

She threw a hand to her mouth to disguise her weeping and made herself leave the room.

Keep going, just keep going.

chapter two

hugh stared down into the bailey. He didn't remember wandering to the window, but most of his body was numb anyway. The ache had started in his chest and spread downward slowly, traversing his limbs into his feet and hands, but then the burn froze, shifting down his spine as if he'd jumped into the Minch. His fingers and toes tingled, then stiffened as if bitten by the frost outside.

It was winter, bitter outside, but that was pretty close to how he'd felt, until everything had iced over, so frigid it actually seemed hot, scorching in its contradiction.

His bones started to shake and even his teeth chattered, despite the fire behind him. The scent of peat moss filled the room, but it was mixed with an aroma that was just his wife.

Somehow, the shuddering got worse. Hugh flexed his hands and arms, but it didn't help.

He couldn't tear his eyes away from the scene below. Two horses stood waiting, hitched to an open-bed cart. A petite blonde woman embraced his wife, her hair lighter in color than Juliette's honey locks. She was dressed warmly, in a dark green cloak with a fur-lined hood she'd just lowered. His sister-by-marriage appeared to share words with Juliette before she returned to the cart, gesturing to his wife, then to the dark-haired man who'd accompanied her into his gates.

Duncan MacLeod hopped off the bench seat.

Hugh's lip curled of its own accord, and a snarl breeched his mouth. His hand landed on the hilt of his sword at the first touch he witnessed. He opened and closed his fingers on the grip, but his feet disobeyed orders to run down there and challenge the MacLeod laird's brother. Or just run him through.

Another man wrapped his wife in a fur. Another man put his hands on her, lifting her gently to the front of the cart. Another man was offering her the comfort he could not, if his rival's gentle expression was any indication.

Hugh wasn't far enough away that it wasn't as plain as the clouded breath from all three of them.

She'd sit next to *him* up front, while his own wife was in the back.

They were taking his Juliette away.

It wasn't against her will.

"I'm leaving, Hugh." The horrid sentence reverberated in his mind, making him freeze all over again. He swallowed, but it helped naught.

Hugh closed his eyes when he heard the *thump thump* of what could only be his Aunt Mab's cane, and the shuffling of her uneven gait.

Juliette had left the door to the laird's quarters open when she'd departed.

"Hugh MacDonald!"

The shout made him flinch, but he didn't move away from the window. He tried to ignore his meddlesome aunt and watched the cart rock with Duncan MacLeod's added weight. The man had indeed taken a seat next to Juliette.

Hugh clenched his jaw.

Duncan took the reins, and even though he couldn't hear anything from his position, Hugh imagined the shout for the horses to dart forward at the moment they did so.

"Hugh MacDonald!"

"Dinnae ye mean, *'my laird?'*" he asked, trying to keep his voice dry. He'd failed. It'd come out a pained crack, betraying how he was feeling. Hugh didn't turn to the woman who'd raised him.

"Nay. I dinnae!" Mab slammed her cane to the floor with a *bang* that echoed.

"Weeel, I am tha laird."

"Ye are a foolish, foolish *lad!*"

He sighed and dragged his hand down his face.

The bailey was empty now. As empty as his heart and soul.

She's really gone. You *drove her away, Hugh MacDonald.*

Guilt and pain swirled low until it jumped up for a bite, and a lump strangled his throat. He remained at the window, looking out. He couldn't deal with himself, let alone Mab. Hugh wished her away, but knew better.

When he'd girded his loins and faced his aunt, he tried to avoid the scowl on her lined face, but her dark eyes speared right through him. That renewed his pain, somehow.

"What. Are. Ye. Doin'?" Mab said the words slowly, each one gaining volume. She panted, she was so angry. Her thin shoulders shook, and her face was crimson, the bright color splotching her cheekbones up to her ears. Her salt and pepper hair was plaited and uncovered, the thick rope swaying with her tremors. Even her dark skirt shook where it rested above the floor.

At least he'd come by his MacDonald temper naturally.

"Sit down, a' fore ye hurt yerself," Hugh admonished.

His aunt narrowed her eyes and brandished her cane like a sword. "Dinnae *ye* try ta order me 'round." With a speed that belied her uneven legs, she crossed the room and smacked his thigh with the staff he'd taken such care to carve for her.

"Ow!" He rubbed his leg as she readied for another strike.

Hugh dodged, but she advanced on him with an agility she shouldn't be capable of.

"Tell me *why* yer lass has left Armadale."

"My marriage dinnae be yer concern." He held his hands up in surrender, then thought better of it. If she hit his bollocks, he'd double over, and he'd just left them unguarded.

Wouldn't put it past her, either.

"Yer marriage? 'Tis verra much *my concern* when tha lass carryin' tha MacDonald heir flees her husband wit'ou' warnin'!"

He stilled and sucked in a breath as anguish spread across his chest all over again.

Juliette really left me.

It hurt to breathe. Hugh's heart cantered and he wanted to clutch something, but didn't want to show weakness, even in front of his auntie.

Mab studied his face and lowered her cane to the stone floor. "Ah, jus' hit ye, did it?"

"What?" he croaked.

"Ye've gone as white as a ghostie."

He swallowed and his knees wobbled.

His aunt's countenance lost some of its ire. "Sit, laddie."

Hugh should be mad it wasn't his idea, but if he

didn't obey, he was going to fall on his arse; in his current attire of a MacDonald plaid, he'd likely bare something Mab had no need to see.

The bed creaked as it protested his weight, and he fought the urge to cradle his head and crush his eyes shut. "'Tis my fault." He winced at the obvious pain in his voice.

Mab snorted. She stood before him; her hands layered on the round knob at the top of her cane. She shook her head, then narrowed her eyes. "I dinnae think any fault lay wit' tha' sweet lass ye wed."

He didn't speak.

"Wha' did ye do, lad?" This was softer.

Emotion stung his eyes. Hugh refused to cry. "I dinnae survive losin' her." This was even more anguished than what he'd managed to say before.

"Ye allowed her ta leave ye." Her expression was placid; she wasn't being accusatory. Just stated the fact that didn't hurt any less.

He shook his head. "Nay. Dinnae be what I'm meanin'."

"Then…wha'?"

Hugh cleared his throat and reached for the right words. The ones he could never say to his wife. He'd tried a few times, especially when Juliette had demanded he talk to her, but he never had been able to.

When she'd cried, he'd plan his own demise.

He averted his gaze from his aunt. "I…I…dinnae be able ta endure losin' her…like Brenna."

The name he *never* said. The wife he never thought about. The bairn who'd never got a chance to be. His son.

Mab's sigh drew his eyes back to her face. His aunt's bottom lip trembled, and she reached for him.

He couldn't deny her, so Hugh wrapped his much larger hand around her gnarled one. He helped her take a seat next to him on the high bed.

"Oh, lad."

Misery washed over him. Her sympathy made him wish she was still shouting. Or hitting his legs with her cane. Maybe even his head.

Should he volunteer his bollocks after all?

Hugh studied his boots and suppressed the shudder in his chest. He tried to square his shoulders but couldn't. He didn't shake Mab off when she squeezed his forearm.

"Lad. Look a' me."

He didn't want to, but damn him, he wouldn't *say* that.

"Hugh."

Sucking in air, he finally mustered the guts to meet her eyes. Words wouldn't cooperate, but he managed not to weep like a lass as she regarded him.

"Did ye tell sweet Juliette a' yer fears?"

Shame and guilt mixed with his agony. "Nay," he croaked.

His aunt blew out a breath and shook her head, making her thick braid dance. "Why no'?"

Hugh didn't answer. He couldn't.

"Juliette dinnae be a' our time, lad, she—"

"I've ruined everythin'."

Mab tugged his wrist until he looked at her again. "Nay, ye dinnae. Ye can go ta her. Speak wit' yer wife, lad. Ye love each other an' are abou' ta have a bairn. Together."

Quivers raced down his spine. *That* was what he couldn't deal with. Week by week, month by month, Juliette's waistline had expanded, revealing the seed he'd planted inside her. Reminding him her passing could be within sight. The bigger her belly got, the closer the impending birth. The closer he was to losing her. He'd not even thought of the bairn.

Hugh couldn't admit that to his aunt. She was more excited about his child than he'd seen her in a long time. *Happy.*

Along with his wife, they'd already prepared the long-unused nursery. A room he couldn't even stomach entering. Not a place for men, anyway.

"I dinnae birth ye, bu' ye know yer like my own, Hugh MacDonald. I raised ye up, alongside my brother. I never wed because ye needed me. I've never asked ye fer anathin'."

Hugh frowned; didn't want to spare her a glance, but when he did, his mouth wobbled at the emotion in her eyes, on her face.

She was still pretty, but his aunt had been stunning back in her day, and many a man had sought her hand.

His father had always left it up to her, and she'd turned down all her suitors.

Because she'd not wanted to leave *him*?

Hugh's mother had died days after his birth. Mab was the only mother he'd ever known, and he loved her. Had he ever told her so?

His father had died when he was one and twenty. His aunt had been there for him then, too. Barely a man, but already a widower, then a laird too young for the sudden responsibilities thrust upon him.

He'd promised his da on his deathbed he'd marry again and provide a MacDonald heir. A vow he'd never intended to fulfill…until Juliette.

Hugh hadn't acknowledged that his aunt had hung her hopes on his gorgeous wife, too.

Guilt wasn't something he needed more of, but it lodged in his gullet, threatening to close it off. He couldn't have spoken a word if he'd had a sword to his back.

"Tha' lass is yer match, my lad. Dinnae let her go. I tol' ye this a 'fore ye wed, bu' now I implore ye, dinnae lose her. Dinnae lose yer bairn. I've ne'er seen ye as happy as I have this past year. I love ye, lad. I love tha' lass, an' I dinnae wan' ta lose either of ye. Or tha' bairn."

He gave in to the urge to close his eyes, and his breath came in short bursts; he had to concentrate on to get any air into his lungs. Hugh's head spun. "Aunt Mab—"

"Juliette has tol' me a' many wondrous things," she said, yanking him from the chaos in his head.

Their gazes collided and held.

"She needs ye, lad. She left a world we dinnae even imagine. Fer ye. Ta be wit' *ye*. An' now she gives ye a bairn. An heir, for ye an' the clan."

"Wondrous things?"

His aunt nodded and swallowed. Her grip on his arm tightened.

"Wha' if…" Hugh took a breath to steady his words. "What if…she asks tha Fae Princess ta take her back ta tha future?"

Mab's dark gaze pinned him. "Ye better hie ta Dunvegan so tha' dinnae happen."

chapter three

The further the bumpy cart got from the gates of Armadale; the more Jules *hurt*. Her heart skipped on its way to overdrive, her stomach knotted, and her baby was swimming on the inside, as if he or she was just as distraught.

Her head fell into her cupped hands, and she tugged her hair. "What am I doing?"

Take me back was on the tip of her tongue, but Claire squeezed her shoulder.

"What you have to."

She couldn't look at her sister, who rode in the back of the cart. Her gaze inadvertently met her brother-in-law's and Jules wanted to wince at the kindness and concern in his very blue eyes.

Her sister had told her a few letters ago; Duncan had needed some convincing to agree to this. He'd probably ranted and raved about taking a man's wife from him—not to mention the former clan-enemy thing they had going for them.

"The first day will be the hardest, but then it'll get easier," Claire said.

Bullshit.

Jules wouldn't get over this for a long, long time, if ever. Couldn't imagine not seeing her husband every day, even if he had been an asshole for months.

She didn't know what to say, so she didn't try. She rocked against the back of the bench seat, resting her hands on her tummy, and willing the baby—and herself—to calm.

"It'll be okay, Jules."

She ignored her sister's words, and the second look Duncan shot her. Couldn't look at either of them, so she studied the terrain.

The ground was covered in dark browns smattered with white. The snow had stopped for now, but the sea still crashed against the loamy shore. It went in and out of view as the wagon followed the ups and downs of the hilly roadway, but she could hear it well enough. The water thundered, like her pulse.

Constant. Violent. Angry. Accusatory.

The wind was frigid, even smelled frozen and promised sleet, yet it had little to do with the shivers that wracked Jules' frame.

Her favorite time on Skye was the spring, when everything was green and bright, and the heather was the pretty bluish-purple that reminded her of Texas bluebonnets and home. The bitterness of a Scottish Hebrides winter was something to get used to. Made what she knew from North Texas pale in comparison. Too bad it was pretty spot on with her feelings today.

Guilt jumped up and latched on—her despair was something she'd brought on herself, wasn't it?

No.

Hugh didn't want their child, so that would *never* work for Jules. He loved her, but he had to love their baby, too. Or she couldn't stay.

In any scenario.

Agony made her double over on the seat.

"Jules? Are you okay?"

Jules crushed her eyes shut as reality washed over her.

She'd *left* her husband.

A sob consumed her throat and pushed its way out. Her vision blurred.

"Jules? Jules, talk to me! Duncan, stop!" Claire said.

"No, no." She managed to wave a hand. "Don't stop. I'm… Just… Let's get to Dunvegan. It's cold."

Her brother-in-law grunted as he encouraged the horses to pick up their former pace. He'd already slowed them at his wife's shout. If he was irritated, he hid it well, but she wouldn't blame him if he was. She'd put him in a position he didn't wholly agree with. He'd only acquiesced because he loved her sister.

Yeah, 'cause I need another man upset with me.

Claire reached forward, rubbing her back. "Of course you're not okay," she murmured. "Just…you're not going into labor or anything, are you?"

Jules managed a snort. "No, I have a few weeks left."

"Good. A cart's no place to have a baby."

She smirked and turned on the bench to face her sister. "1676 is no place to have a baby."

Claire echoed her smirk. "I did it in 1673. You'll be fine. I'm about to do it again."

"You are?"

Her sister's expression turned sheepish. "Aye. It's not a secret, but with everything going on with you and Hugh, I didn't want to bot—"

"Claire! I'm always up for good news!" Jules was able to smile genuinely and awkwardly hugged her sister, the back of the bench seat between them. "Congrats, baby sis!"

Duncan was grinning when she spared him a glance. "Alana says 'tis another lad."

Claire sighed over dramatically.

Jules found herself laughing. It felt good not to be mired down in despair, even if it likely wouldn't last.

"I want a girl," her sister mumbled.

Duncan chuckled. "Then, *mò gradh*, we shall have ta make 'nother. I always try ta give my wife wha' she wants."

Claire blushed, and Jules shook her head. How her

sister could be embarrassed after four years of marriage and a three-year-old son was beyond her. However, she was adorable, her green eyes bright.

"Thanks for coming to get me, you guys." She breathed through the sadness re-descending and tried to fight it off.

The couple fell silent, but her brother-in-law nodded.

Jules shouldn't be envious that Duncan was happy Claire was pregnant again, and could joke about future children, instead of rejecting the one they'd made with love. She needed a distraction. "So, how pregnant are you? Alana told you with magic what the baby is?"

Relief danced across her sister's pretty face. She nodded. "Aye, with magic. She can do the same for you if you want. About four months."

Conversation faded in and out as they rode toward the MacLeod stronghold, and for the most part Jules was able to ban her husband from her thoughts. She looked forward to seeing her sister's family, especially her nephew, Lachlan, as well as the other kids.

Duncan's brother, Alex, had two, thirteen-year-old Angus, and two-year-old Alexandria, whom everyone called Lexi, due to Claire's tendency to nickname people. Duncan's sister Janet had a little boy who was almost one, Liam. All four of the children had dark hair—despite all of them having one fair-haired parent—and looked more like siblings than cousins.

She couldn't help but think about her own baby.

With Jules' luck, her son or daughter would be the spitting image of Hugh. Somehow that hurt all over again.

"C'mon, Jules. We're here." Claire's voice was low and broke into her painful musings.

She should thank her sister.

"If we're lucky, Mairi already has lunch ready."

Jules nodded and let Duncan help her down from the cart. She didn't say it, but she didn't have much of an appetite.

♡ ♡ ♡

The next morning came too soon. Agony and tears took her over when Jules woke up in a bed that wasn't her own.

She'd really done it.

I left Hugh.

It hadn't been some horrible nightmare.

Like him, she'd been married once before. However, leaving her cheating bastard of an ex-husband hadn't been a regret, it'd been justified. She'd cried, of course, but Jules had gotten over him even before the divorce was final. Hadn't looked back.

Until Hugh.

Leaving her second husband—the love of her life—was different.

Claire burst into the guestroom she'd been given yesterday after the midday meal. Her sister had a tray of food; the scent of fresh bread teased her nose and perked Jules' senses awake. She set the full trencher on what passed for a desk, not far from the bed, and bustled to the heavy drapes.

Light bathed the room, bringing it to life as if it too had just woken. Unfortunately, spotlighting this room just made her more miserable.

This room was the one she'd agreed to marry Hugh in. On this bed, she'd given herself to him to seal the promise. Jules should've asked her sister to put her in a different guestroom.

She wiped her face and prayed Claire wouldn't notice she'd been crying.

Clan MacLeod had welcomed her back, like they had when she'd arrived last year, but she could only take so much of their concern. Alex, Duncan's twin, and the Laird MacLeod had told her she could stay as long as she needed, which had just put her into her thousandth fit of tears.

She'd eaten supper with only her sister in this room, but the rest of Claire's wonderful loving family hovered like they always did. The last thing Jules needed right now was to be smothered, but she did smile when one of Duncan's cousins, Cormac, threatened to beat Hugh up for her; she only had to say *aye*, the big man had vowed.

Her tummy growled as the food wafted further into the room, and her baby did what felt like a backflip. She sat up in the borrowed bed, and her bladder stood up and shouted, *hello*.

"Gooooood mornin'!" Her sister grinned. She'd been in seventeenth century Scotland for four years, so Claire's accent had gone from modern-day Texan to Scottish lass—or really, something that fluctuated in between.

"I have to pee."

She paused by the bed. "TMI."

Jules snorted. "That's not TMI. I can give you some TMI if you want. My boobs are killing me, I ache in other—"

Claire giggled and shook her head. "Damn, I missed you, big sis. Sometimes letters don't do it."

"Miss me later, can you help me up?"

"Of course."

Her sister helped her out of bed, and to handle her morning business—definitely a downside to the seventeenth century.

"I brought you breakfast, because I assumed you wouldn't want to be social this morning, but Janet and Alana want to see you when you're ready."

"Appreciate it. Really." Jules couldn't take overprotective MacLeods any more this morning than she could yesterday. Not yet anyway.

Claire nodded and pulled the padded chair out from the desk, practically pushing her down into it.

"I'm pregnant, not an invalid, you know."

"You've been through a trauma." She took the opposite seat, broke the small loaf of bread open, and handed her half, along with a bowl of honey butter.

"God, no. Please don't."

Her sister's gaze was somber as she regarded her. "It's true, Jules."

"I don't need you cop-talking me. Or worse, sounding like a therapist." Jules had been a detective and had said the trauma crap to many a victim of various crimes. Especially when a woman lost her husband, no matter how it'd happened.

Claire sighed and popped a piece of cheese into her mouth. "Fine. I'll leave things alone for now. Just take it one day at a time."

"Thank you." She took a bite of bread and closed her eyes. "This is awesome. Don't tell Mab I said this, but Mairi's honey butter is way better than hers."

A ghost of a smile played on her sister's lips, but she didn't speak. She concentrated a bit too hard on the food in front of her.

"What, Claire?"

"Nothing."

"Bullshit. Just say what you want to say. Frankly, I'm shocked you're not all like, *'Go back to Armadale, Hugh loves you.'*"

Her sister blew out a breath, averted her gaze, then looked back at her. "I wouldn't say that to you right now."

"I heard the *yet*."

"I know he's been an asshole, but I *do* believe he loves you."

He does. He told me when I walked out on him.

Jules' bottom lip wobbled, and her appetite dissipated, despite the yummy honey butter and the rest of the bread in front of her.

"Aww, dammit. I didn't mean to make you cry." Claire closed her eyes and sighed again.

She sucked in her cheek, bit down, and looked anywhere but at her sister.

"Look, bottom line, you need to be here, you be here. Even if Alex didn't okay it, I'd find a way. You're my sister and I love you. But Hugh's baby is... *Hugh's baby*. His firstborn, his heir, especially if you're having a boy. You can't stay here forever. You know it even if you won't *say* it. You don't have the luxury of rockin' the single motherhood thing in this century."

"I know," Jules whispered. "Can you lay off the reality check, please? At least for now? I just... I just..." Tears spilled, hot on her cheeks, and the baby shifted inside her, pressing on her organs with a jolting discomfort that felt like revenge. Jules winced and shifted on the chair.

"Jesu," Claire said, sounding just like her husband — or Hugh. She was on her feet in seconds and wrapped her arms around her. "Now *I'm* the asshole."

"Yes, you are." Her words were muffled against her sister's shoulder. "You just took me in; only to say you'd put a pregnant chick out on the street — or in the field, around here."

Claire pulled back, but amusement darted across her pretty face. "Wow, you're laying it on thick, arencha?"

Their gazes locked and they were silent for a moment, but then they broke into giggles.

Jules' emotions were all over the place, but it felt good to laugh with her sister.

Conversation fell to the wayside as Claire returned to her seat and they both ate, but the heavy words—the truth—played on a loop in her head.

What am I going to do?

"I could…go home." She regretted the blurt as soon as it'd breached her lips. Partially because Jules didn't want to go back to the future—she wanted Hugh to want her and the baby—and partially because of the look that darted across her sister's face.

"What?" Claire demanded.

"I didn't mean it." She shook her head.

"Well, you said it, so you kinda meant it." Her sister's fair brow was drawn, tight and accusatory.

Jules sucked in a breath and closed her eyes. "I really didn't. I mean…the thought crossed my mind once or twice. He…hurt me. You *know* he did. But…my life is here. My life is Hugh." She clenched her jaw to stop more tears. Saying the words and coming to terms with walking away from him warred inside her. "God knows what they think happened to us in Texas, but—"

"Before you got here, I thought about you all the time. *You* were my only regret. Then…you came, and fell in love, and *stayed*."

"I know, Claire. I don't want the future, except seventeenth century speaking. I just want Hugh to want his child as much as he wants me."

"I know." Her sister's expression lost its irritated, defensive edge.

Their many letters detailed Hugh's neglect of her over the course of her pregnancy. Claire had first stood up for Jules' husband, citing his past losses, but as the months went on and he continued to ignore her, denying there was an issue, her little sister had gone mama-bear on her husband — in writing anyway.

Although, given the chance, she wouldn't put it past Claire to give him a tongue lashing. Jules had taught her all she knew, of course.

"What would you have done if Duncan hadn't wanted Lachlan? What if he didn't want the baby you're carrying now?" The more she spoke aloud of how Hugh felt the more her voice wobbled, until she barely held the sob at bay.

Her sister looked down. "I don't know, Jules."

Jules bit the inside of her cheek again and looked away. Her gut roiled, and even though she'd long since been done with morning sickness, she contemplated vomiting.

"I know what could cheer you up!" Even in the chair, her sister fairly bounced in her ladies' slippers. Her expression was so hopeful that Jules would buy it, she couldn't help indulging her.

"What?" She tried not to roll her eyes and reclined

in the chair.

"We'll celebrate Valentine's Day!" Her sister's green eyes lit up and she leaned forward, her flaxen locks swaying around her lap. "Twenty-first century style!"

"Right. That would *so* cheer me up." She'd just lost the only Valentine she'd ever want. Jules bit down until her teeth ached and tried to take comfort in her baby's movements, resting her hand on her belly.

Remorse darted across Claire's face, as if she'd read her like a book. Knowing her sister, she probably had. "Damn. I'm a *jerk*. I…didn't think about it that way. I'm sorry. I just want to distract you."

"It's okay. I guess I have to get used to it." Her voice wavered, even to her own ears.

Claire sighed for the third time and darted back to her, enveloping her in another hug Jules couldn't fight. She needed the comfort.

"It'll be okay. I thought we weren't gonna talk about reality checks?"

"But it won't be okay, and I need to deal with that. Maybe you were right about that." Her voice was weak, and it wasn't because she was against her sister's slender body.

Claire pulled back. Her expression said she didn't agree, but she didn't comment about Hugh again.

Thank God.

"When we were little, *you* were my Valentine. So, this year, I can be yours."

Jules snorted. "Isn't Valentine's Day just a religious holiday around here? It's called something else… It's too early — like over a hundred years — for the hearts-and-cupids thing."

Claire winked. "Does it matter?"

"Yeah, I think it does. The not changing history thing, and all that."

"Nah, it won't matter in the scheme of things! We'll throw a party and make paper hearts or something. We can wear red. The kids will love it, too! Alana and Janet will help, I'm sure of it. We have a few days until the fourteenth!"

Yes, because I'm so freakin' feeling like partying.

With another look at her sister's expectant expression, Jules didn't have the heart to tear down the attempt to cheer her up. There was no reason to hurt Claire's feelings, too. And shit, it might help; who the hell knew? "Fine. We'll celebrate Valentine's Day our way." She tried to muster a smile for her sibling.

Her sister's face lit up again, making her seem years younger. "Yay, Jules! It'll help, I promise."

Yeah, I doubt that.

She forced a nod as Claire flitted from the room with the empty trencher.

Jules sighed and tried not to give into more tears.

chapter four

The soft knock on the door jolted Jules from a half-asleep state.

"Oh, I didn't mean to wake you. I can come back."

"No, no, come in." She sat up and tried to smile.

Her sister's *'let's celebrate Valentine's Day'* thing had been a go from first light; they'd spent the morning in the solar, making parchment hearts and even a heart garland or two. She didn't want to know what the red and pink dyes were made from.

Seeing the children laugh and play — and mostly ignore the four women and two servant girls that were interested in *the day* — had been heartening, but Jules had tired out and snuck away for a nap.

Claire's sister-in-law, Alana, slipped into the room and shut the door. "How are you?"

Jules fought a yawn and the constant depression. "I've been better."

"The bairn?" She crossed the distance and perched on the bed next to her.

"No, the baby's fine."

The former Fae princess smiled. "May I?"

"Sure." Jules couldn't look away from the gentle violet eyes appraising her.

Alana's expression was just as soft, and she fought tears.

Again.

She didn't want someone else to look at her like that. She bit her bottom lip and tried to avert her gaze, but couldn't.

The touch was warm on her distended tummy, even through her clothing, and Alana's hands began to glow as she checked her over with magic. She didn't speak, but she looked at Jules' stomach with a slight smile curving her full mouth.

"The bairn is healthy," she said finally.

Relief and elation washed over Jules, but it battled with the sadness she was coming to loathe. Hugh wasn't here, at her side, to hear this news.

It wasn't like he wanted to be, either.

He might love *her*, but he didn't love or want their child.

The knowledge haunted her.

"That's good to hear," she forced out, but her words tremored.

The princess sighed and met her gaze. The radiant white glow in her hands faded, and she reached for Jules' forearm. She squeezed, and her purple eyes settled into impossibly sincere and soft again. "I can assure you there's nothin' wrong with your bairn, and I—or my cousin—could likely heal any problems, but I cannot do anythin' to heal your heart, and for that, I am sorry." Her formal tone mixed with Highland brogue was as endearing as she was, but it didn't stop Jules' tears.

She tried to blink them away, but it was no use. Soon they cascaded down her cheeks. Looking anywhere but at the princess didn't help.

"All is well, or *'twill* be." Alana kept her voice low. "I have an idea of something 'twill make you smile."

Jules snorted. "Not likely."

The princess waited for their eyes to meet again and smiled. It lit up her face, and Jules was awestruck by her beauty, alabaster skin, long white-blonde hair, and those eyes, even though she'd known the Fae woman for a year now.

"If I were my husband, I'd offer you a wager on that." Alana winked.

Jules couldn't keep from smiling, but it was tiny. "Okay, then. Let me have it."

"Well, first I shall ask, would you like to know what your bairn is?"

"As in, boy or girl?"

She nodded.

Yes, Jules wanted to know, but she'd always imagined Hugh would want to know, too. She banished the renewed pain and nodded.

Alana's smile slid into a grin. "'Tis a lass."

Her heart skipped. More tears were born, but this time they were more happy than sad. "A baby girl?" Jules smiled genuinely, even if it was wobbly. "A little girl."

Would her husband be disappointed their first child wasn't a boy?

Her joy stalled.

Alana squeezed her hand. "Do not think about him for now. Focus on the wee lass 'twill soon be in your arms."

"How did you know?" she choked out.

"I can't read minds like Xander, but I can feel your emotions, and you're all over the place, so 'twas a fortunate guess. Try to stay calm, for your daughter's sake."

"Easier said than done."

Her eyes held so much feeling *for* Jules, her breath evaporated.

"I'm sorry." Jules shrugged, then swiped at her face and sniffled.

Alana flitted across the room only to return with a handkerchief from the vanity. "You have nothing to be sorry about, Lady MacDonald."

Jules startled, and the *thank you* on the tip of her tongue dissipated. "Just...Jules...please." She didn't need another reminder of Hugh.

Not like she didn't have a constant one, anyway, growing inside her.

The princess' expression flipped to contrite as she retook a seat on the bed. "I'm sorry for further upsetting you. I meant no harm."

"You're fine, really. This…" She took a breath. "I know my…situation is…unusual. Women don't…leave their husbands in this century." Jules fought the urge to crumple.

"I don't blame you, and I don't think anyone else does, either. Even the menfolk. Hugh MacDonald is a hard man to deal with; I can't imagine trying to love him." Alana's pretty face had sadness stamped all over it. She was no doubt still feeling everything Jules was.

"I do!" Jules blurted. "I love him so much."

"I can feel it. 'Tis why you hurt so badly." The princess squeezed her hand. "I have faith it'll work itself out. Do not fash yourself now."

She didn't have the guts to disagree or ask how.

"Jules, are you okay?" Claire slipped into the room.

Alana stood and smiled. "She is. The bairn is well, and a wee lassie."

"A girl!" Her sister clapped. "I'm so jealous!" She rubbed her barely showing tummy, her mouth curved up. "I want a little girl like Lexi!"

The princess laughed. "My daughter would also appreciate a lassie to play with, instead of the two lads she has."

Claire grinned. "Lachlan does enjoy pestering her."

"Liam does his fair share, now that he's walking," Alana said of her other nephew.

They both laughed.

Jules tried to push away the envy that settled over her from watching the two women interact. Her sister had two women to commiserate with, raise her babies with, and be *friends* with. She didn't have anyone like that at Armadale. Mab was great, but Hugh's aunt was in her sixties.

Claire's sisters-in-law were lovely. Even though Jules had kind of been forced to socialize all morning, seeing them laugh and talk together, working on her sister's silly party, had been something wonderful.

They were a team, and they'd tried their best to include Jules' doldrums-stricken self. She might be blood to Claire, but they seemed closer to her than she felt.

She couldn't help but watch them parent their children, too. Jules could learn a lot from them. She was older than Claire and Janet, but they were both experienced mothers.

Alana knew what she was doing, too, but she was probably older than Hugh's aunt. Fae lived twice—or more—than the human lifespan, so she didn't look a day over thirty. It'd be rude to ask, so Jules would just have to wonder about the princess' real age.

Jules was nervous. Had never really planned for kids—she'd been a cop, and serially single. Until Hugh. Then she'd wanted them. She'd wanted *his* babies.

Too bad he didn't.

They'd be like any new parents—trial and error—but without modern conveniences. Or really *any* conveniences. No drugs for the birth, either.

And as of right now, I'll be on my own with all this stuff.

Jules stifled a moan of misery and pressed against the pillows.

Alana threw her a worried glance. "Don't fash about anything, Jules," she repeated.

The brightness in Claire's expression fell. "What's wrong?"

She shook her head and gestured helplessly. "Nothing and everything. I'll be fine."

The two women exchanged a look, but neither contradicted her.

Silence filled the space, but two sets of eyes regarded her with all sorts of concern she wanted to ignore.

"Maybe I should just go home. Back to Armadale," Jules blurted, adding the MacDonald stronghold so her sister wouldn't think she meant the future and flip out.

Claire took the princess' former seat on the bed beside her and grabbed her hand. Her green eyes were somber. "If you want to."

Jules closed her eyes. "I don't know what I want."

Liar.

She wanted Hugh, and as things stood, that was part of the problem.

♡ ♥ ♡

Hugh stalked through the great hall, and the two servant lasses cleaning the vast place scattered.

One squeaked, the other squealed, even though neither was close enough to him to be considered in his way.

There was a clatter as one of them dropped something, but he didn't stop to chide her. She'd likely burst into tears, and he wasn't in the mood.

If *black* was even a mood. It was the only color he could see.

More accurately, he lacked a mood. A feeling. *Any* feeling—singular or plural. His body wasn't his anymore. His nerves had gone numb the day Juliette had left him and had stayed that way.

Hugh had even gone for an icy—literally—dip in the sea, and it'd done nothing except make his teeth chatter and his skin bluish. Re-donning clothes he'd taken off for his winter swim hadn't been able to dry or warm him much. He'd come home shivering—which in turn had made his aunt fuss until he'd walked away from her. He'd have to deal with that fallout later.

His black stallion had refused to get wet. Dubh had stared from the shoreline, the wind in his mane and tail, almost as if he was confirming his master had finally lost his mind.

At least the steed was loyal—he'd waited for him.

What Hugh had hoped to gain from his self-baptism was a mystery. The move hadn't fixed his numbness, or the hole where his heart used to be.

She's still gone.

He stomped up the stairs to his ledger room.

Hugh had assumed—hoped…mentally begged?—that Juliette would come back to him after a day or so. It'd been *three*. There was no sign of his wife.

A part of him hadn't doubted her seriousness.

A part of him was angry, but the hurt overwhelmed that, which was probably the cause of his broken nerves. Disbelief was there, too, but only a tad because he knew his wife well.

"She ran ou' of patience ta put up wit' yer shite, Hugh MacDonald." He shook his head and chided himself some more.

Juliette had told him that vulgar phrase on more than one occasion, and he'd always laughed. Which would raise her ire, they'd argue some more, and then make love—forcing it all to go away.

His wife talked to him as no one else would dare—one of the many reasons he loved her.

She's still gone.

Hugh yanked the chair out from behind his desk and restrained himself from throwing it against the wall to watch it splinter. Or he could just toss it into the lit hearth. He could burn the wood, but then he'd have to deal with Mab for wasting a perfectly good chair—and she'd bemoan the expense to replace it.

He gritted his teeth and took a seat.

There were some scrolls on his desk that his steward needed him to look at, but he couldn't deal with being the laird at the moment. Or in the near future.

"This isn't about love." Juliette's words bounced off the walls of his aching head. Or maybe the walls and ceiling of the ledger room.

Since when did he concern himself with tender feelings?

Since Juliette, you sodding fool.

Hugh couldn't lie to himself. Not about Juliette. He *did* love her. More than his own life.

So, what's wrong with you, then, Hugh MacDonald?

His aunt had hollered at him to go get her multiple times a day since she'd left. Mab had told him to talk to Juliette. Explain how he was feeling—speak of his fear, and though his aunt hadn't said so, she'd implied, accept responsibility for hurting his wife, making Juliette want to leave him in the first place, and generally for being an arse.

He needed to.

Why hadn't he left already?

Because Juliette was in the right.

She likely needed some time to herself as well.

She's had three days. Go to her, wretch.

Was he just a coward?

Hugh couldn't answer himself, for fear of the truth.

He'd treated her badly. Pushing her away like he'd never done before, but he couldn't look at her growing belly. The bairn's presence was a constant reminder of how he could lose Juliette. How he'd already lost one wife and child, and he'd not gotten the chance to love the shy lass his father had ordered him to marry when he'd been twenty years old to her six and ten.

Many times, Juliette had referred to *him* as the love of her life.

She was the same for him.

Hugh swallowed. There was a brick in his throat, and it was slowly working its way down to his gut, hardening every part of him as it went. Agony spread across his chest and down, but at least he was feeling something.

"Hugh MacDonald."

He didn't want to look at the doorway—nor did he look up as he heard her uneven step cross the room.

Go away, auntie, was on the tip of his tongue, but since his little dip in the sea, he didn't dare. Mab was already angry with him. He was looking at a beating with her cane at best as it was. On the other hand, maybe *that* could make him feel better.

"Have ye come ta yer senses?"

"Regardin'?" Hugh tried to keep his voice dry but failed. The word came out like the painful crack it was.

"Yer. Wife."

When he mustered the bollocks to look at the woman who'd raised him, her dark eyes were narrowed. A constant expression on her face as of late, but he couldn't risk pointing that out, either.

Hugh sighed. "Will ye leave me be, woman?"

"Nay." His aunt's voice was deceptively calm.

"Nay?" he yelled.

"Nay. No' until yer lass has returned."

He wanted to growl and scream, but like his Juliette, that rarely had an effect on Aunt Mab.

"Ye love tha' lass. Yer bairn will be here any day now. Go get what's yers."

"I do love tha' lass."

And I need to go get her. Beg her forgiveness.

Silence fell, as if his aunt hadn't expected him to say that.

When their gazes collided, a dark bushy eyebrow was cocked high.

"They do belong ta me," Hugh said. He stood. Cleared his throat but avoided Mab's eyes again. He moved past his meddlesome aunt.

He wouldn't contemplate what he'd do if Juliette turned him away.

She wouldn't. She couldn't.

Right?

Hugh wouldn't voice his worries—even though his aunt would likely reassure him his wife wouldn't deny him. The lass loved *him*, too.

Tremors chased each other down his spine, but he

ignored them. He'd crawl in front of every MacLeod if he had to. He'd get his lass—his family—back.

Maybe he should thank his aunt, but he wouldn't give her satisfaction for something he'd decided for himself already.

He didn't need a final push. Hugh loved his wife, and he was going to get her back.

"Where ye goin'?" Mab's voice made him jump.

She'd shocked his head into silence—for now.

"Ta order the lads ta ready my horse."

Anger creased his aunt's brow. "Ye dinnae be run—"

"I'm goin' ta Dunvegan," Hugh whispered.

She tilted her head and leaned in, framing the shell of her ear with gnarled fingers. "Speak up, lad, my hearin' dinnae be wha' it used ta be."

He snorted.

The woman wouldn't allow him to lie to her, but *she* could lie to him?

His wife's gorgeous face danced in from his memories. He sucked in a breath, and his heart skipped. "I will hie ta Dunvegan."

Mab grinned.

Hugh frowned and said nothing. Tried not to stomp from the ledger room, lest she call him a foolish laddie again.

Chapter Five

The Valentine's Day party was in full swing in the great hall. Alana, Xander, and young Angus had pooled their magical talents to conjure red flowers, and they were draped everywhere, along with Claire's parchment garlands and hearts that hung on anything standing still. The only thing missing was glitter, but it was better left in the future.

Each of the long tables had been decorated, too, with red and pink tablecloths and a flowery centerpiece on top. Jules was pretty sure the colors had been magically infused into the fabric, and probably weren't permanent.

Claire had gone overboard, but that wasn't a shocker. She'd even joked about wanting a disco ball—another thing better left where it'd been born.

The atmosphere was lighthearted and fun. Loving,

even. Family.

Jules felt guilty for just sitting like a lump on a log at the head table while everyone laughed and talked around her, but she wasn't interested in any of it—or the food on her plate. It'd long gone cold and everyone else had already eaten.

The happily married couples around her—Alex and Alana, Xander and Janet, as well as Duncan and Claire—made her insides wither, and watching them was difficult. Especially since her sister had explained what Valentine's Day meant in their time. Commercially speaking anyway.

Jules snorted. Her younger sister had always pouted if she'd not gotten a gift on the big love day— of course she'd always cried if she'd been single on her favorite holiday.

Funny how fate had made Claire land in a time where the day didn't exist as they'd know it in the future, and her soulmate was a big strong Highlander mostly unfamiliar with being romantic.

Although Jules had to give it to Duncan. The guy could be sweet, and he did love her sister. Would do anything for her and their son—and it'd be the same for her nephew that wasn't born yet.

Jules had to look away when the laird got down on one knee and presented a red rose to his princess, then asked her to dance to the slow song the MacLeod bards were playing on instruments and singing from the corner of the room.

The kids laughed and played, and at least that distracted her. Her little nephew had brought her a red flower and a paper heart with her name on it, and she'd been able to smile genuinely. When Lachlan had wanted to sit with her, and stood on the chair next to hers, only to lean over and kiss her cheek, she almost lost it again. Tried to avoid his huge sapphire eyes, because the three-year-old didn't understand why his aunt was sad.

She'd soon sent him back to Claire's arms, and her sister danced with the little boy while they both shared loud kisses and giggles as she swayed.

Duncan watched them with obvious affection for only a moment, then joined them, wrapping his arms around them both.

Angus, Alex and Alana's son, was still at the table with Jules. He leaned over and covered her hand in his, a gesture much too old and sincere for his age.

Jules was compelled to look into his eyes—also blue, the most common MacLeod trait.

"'Twill all be well, Aunt Jules."

She wasn't really his aunt, but all the kids who could talk called her that. Jules tried not to look down or away, but her neck and cheeks heated.

How could she argue with a kid who couldn't know about everything going on?

"I've seen it," he asserted. Then Angus smiled, and looked so much like his father and uncle he could've been a clone.

Seen it?

Jules wouldn't ask aloud. She'd been told the laird's son had visions—premonitions—or whatever, and magic was real and all that, so she was afraid to hope he wasn't just trying to make her feel better. "Well, thanks, I guess."

Angus nodded and went to his baby sister when she whined for him. The boy swept her up into his arms until the tiny girl giggled, her dark curls flying.

Her back gave a twinge, so she straightened in the chair. When that didn't help, Jules gained her feet, rubbing the spot.

The discomfort spread, rippling around to the front of her stomach, and she gasped. No one was at the table with her, and she didn't want to try to navigate the three dais stairs on her own. She gripped the back of the chair and whimpered when the pain worsened.

"Jules?"

Claire's voice washed relief over her. Thank God her sister was keeping an annoyingly close eye on her. *This time* she was grateful, anyway.

"Claire," she panted.

Her sister set her son down and lifted her olive-green skirts, jogging up the steps to join her. Took her hand. "What's wrong? What happened?"

"I…don't know…but…"

Liquid rushed down Jules' legs, smacking onto the dais planks, soaking her legs and her dress. She blew out air. She hadn't just lost her bladder, so—

"Oh crap, your water just broke!" Her sister's green eyes went wide. "Why didn't you tell me you're in labor? Have you been having contractions?"

"What? My water… I didn't… I'm not?" Panic hit and tightened her chest. Jules hung onto Claire's hand for dear life. "Am I? I haven't had any pain until right now…"

"Does your back hurt?" Her sister looked over her shoulder without waiting for an answer. "Janet, Alana, her water just broke. It's baby time."

"Yes, my back…baby time?" Jules sputtered.

Both women nodded, and Janet handed her toddler son to his father, Xander.

Alana slipped from the laird's arms and came toward them. "Janet and I will bring what we need. We'll meet you in the guestroom."

"Duncan, can you help with her?" Claire called to her husband.

"Wait. What?" Jules' head spun.

It's not time.

It couldn't be time. It wasn't time.

She still had two weeks. Right?

"It'll be okay, Jules." Her sister's voice didn't comfort her.

It's not okay. Hugh's not here.

Without a word, Duncan swung her up into his arms.

Jules was caught off guard and clutched at him. Breath fled her lungs, and her middle was now radiating pain, like a slow fire spreading wider.

When she met her brother-in-law's gaze, he smirked.

"Sorry, I dinnae mean ta alarm ye. Hold onta me, lass. I'll no' drop ye."

A contraction took all her attention, so Jules forced a nod and let him hold her—as if she had a choice. She wove her arms around his neck.

His body was hard—not unlike Hugh's—and Duncan was warm. She wanted to burrow into her sister's husband so she'd stop hurting, and maybe her head would stop its ride on the *Tilt-A-Whirl.*

"Oh, God," Jules moaned.

She was barely aware of Duncan climbing the stairs and kicking the door to her guestroom open. He set her gently on the bed and straightened.

Claire was on his heels but came right to the side of the bed. "I think you were in labor all day. Did your back hurt? That's how it started for me with Lachlan."

Jules ignored her sister and made eye contact with her brother-in-law, who hovered near the end of the bed now. "Hugh. I need Hugh."

"Jules—"

"I need my husband," she gritted through her teeth as another contraction—or maybe it was the same one—tried to monopolize all her attention.

"Jules!" Claire barked.

"I'll…never…forgive myself if he misses…this," she breathed.

Maybe he *won't forgive me, either.*

Jules made tight fists of the bed linens. Her knuckles were the same pale color as she panted through the agony.

"Yer sister is right, *mò gradh.* Her husband should be here. 'Tis his bairn, too. His heir." Duncan's expression softened as he regarded them both.

Jules relaxed back into the pillows her sister had propped at her back and blew out a breath as the pain finally released her.

"I'm not arguing about that," Claire said. She shook her head, making her flaxen locks dance. "I just don't know how much time we have, since you didn't realize you were in labor. Let me see what's keeping Alana; she's delivered more babies than me." She hurried from the guestroom without another word.

It should be surreal that her sister had delivered babies *at all*, but they lived in the seventeenth century, and a woman had to do what a woman had to do.

"I'll go fetch Laird MacDonald." Duncan shook his head, grinning. "'Tis the first MacDonald heir e'er ta be born a' Dunvegan, fer sure."

She managed a smirk for the big Highlander. "I bet so, and it's gonna piss him off. But... I need him."

Duncan offered a curt nod, but his eyes said he'd understood more than her words. "I'll be quick abou' it, lass."

"Thanks, Duncan," she whispered, but he was already gone.

chapter six

ubh tossed his head and hoofed the ground, then shifted his weight and nickered.

Hugh barely paid his dear steed any notice even as he swayed with the horse's movements. The reins lay loose in one palm, and even if his stallion was protesting, he wouldn't take off without command.

He couldn't tear his eyes off the MacLeod stronghold from his place high up on the ridge. They'd been standing there for hours that felt like days.

Mab had told him to go get his wife, and he wanted to. *Needed* to. However, after riding out, he'd wandered Skye more than coming directly to the MacLeods.

The wind was bitter, and it was snowing big fat lazy flakes. Hugh could hear his aunt's voice in his head, chiding him that he'd catch his death, but he couldn't bring himself to care. His body was mostly numb again, like it'd been since his dip in the sea, and since she'd left him.

He must've lost his bollocks somewhere along the journey because he couldn't go forward toward Dunvegan, and he *wouldn't* go home. Not without her, anyway.

Juliette.

His wife was safe inside those walls. Residing with a clan that wasn't his.

Safe from me?

Hugh swallowed and called himself every name he could think of—in Gaelic and English. Even some curses common in the far future Juliette had taught him, but never around Mab. His aunt didn't like that kind of talk, especially from the Lady of Armadale.

If he closed his eyes, Hugh could see his wife's face, and recall when she'd quoted her favorites, grinning like they had a secret. His chest ached, and every breath was like a dagger, as if his stallion was seated upon his torso pushing the blade deeper.

Dubh backed up and stepped forward.

Hugh wobbled, then tightened his grip on the reins. He sat taller, re-centering himself. "What's botherin' ye, laddie?" He paused and tilted his head to one side when his mount whinnied and pranced.

Thundering hooves echoed, but it wasn't more than one horse, unless his ears deceived him. Their position obscured the gates of his rival's vast wall, but obviously a rider had just left from where he couldn't see. They should be visible in moments, and Dubh had heard them first.

The horse was white—and he'd seen it before.

His stallion needed little encouragement to head back to the road they were only ten or so feet above; he practically cantered down the ridge to level ground. Hugh reined Dubh in more than his horse liked, but he'd not want them to be run over.

The man hollered when he'd spotted them and slowed in plenty of time to avoid a collision.

Surprise washed over Hugh when the rider straightened and lowered the hood of his gray mantel.

"Hugh MacDonald!"

Only the smile on Duncan MacLeod's beardless face stalled his demand for the respect—and honorific—he'd left off Hugh's name. The man shouldn't have greeted him so casually, even if they were brothers-by-marriage.

He scowled. "MacLeod."

Amusement darted across his broad face, and he kneed his steed closer to Dubh. "Wha're ye doin' lurkin' 'round my lands?"

"Yer *brother's* lands," he barked.

Duncan arched a dark eyebrow but didn't say anything.

Contrition—but not guilt—crept up from the pit of his stomach. Even if Hugh didn't like this man much, he shouldn't be a wretch. In the very least, Duncan had cared for Juliette. He frowned and cleared his throat. "Ye know well why I've come."

Blue eyes studied him, and Duncan raised his chin. "Aye."

"If ye say 'twas abou' time, I'll knock ye off yer horse," he snarled.

The man's chuckle made him narrow his eyes, but when Duncan shook his head and threw his palms high, all Hugh could do was curse under his breath.

What's so damn funny?

"I dinnae say anathin." The man squared his shoulders, and their gazes locked. "I am, however, grateful ta find ye here. 'Twill be a shorter ride home."

He reared back and gripped Dubh's reins tighter, shifting on his saddle-less back. Hugh *knew* what Duncan would say before his rival spoke.

"'Tis yer lass' time."

Panic washed over him, and he squeezed his thighs around his horse so he wouldn't slip off the stallion's back and tumble to the frozen ground on his arse. He swallowed—twice. "Is she—"

Duncan was close enough to grab his forearm. "MacDonald?"

When Hugh found the man's eyes again, he wanted to order him to go to hell, because Duncan MacLeod had never regarded him with concern before. However, looking at him at least gave Hugh something to focus on. He couldn't even muster the energy to shove his hand off.

"She's askin' fer ya. Sent me ta get ye."

Hugh blinked. As if he hadn't understood the words. His insides had, because his heart galloped, and his gut clenched. "Juliette," he whispered.

"Aye, tha lass ye connived inta marryin' ye."

He growled and ignored Duncan's laugh.

"Let's hie to Dunvegan, my laird. Yer bairn is comin'."

My bairn.

Hugh released a breath. His head spun a little less, but it didn't help the agony in his chest. "I dinnae…lose her," he blurted.

Duncan paused.

When he had the bollocks to look at the man, his rival's dark brow was knitted tight. He steeled himself for some comment about Brenna. It wasn't a secret how he'd lost his first wife and child.

Hugh tried not to wince.

"Ye should tell *her* tha'."

The comment wasn't what he'd expected, but still nothing he wanted to hear—or could deal with. He forced a nod. It was all he had.

"My brother's wife says yer wife an' child are healthy. 'Tis no reason ta fear the birth will be difficult." The man made his mouth a line and nodded curtly.

Hugh appreciated that Duncan hadn't commented on the past. He echoed the nod and managed not to give into the hovering sob like a lassie. News that Juliette and the bairn—*his* bairn—were well eased him,

if only a little. He hoped it wasn't too good to be true.
"Does...does..."

Duncan looked at him expectantly but waited for
him to work his thoughts out.

"The laird's wife. 'Tis rumored ta be—"

"Ye ken well 'tis true. Why do ye ask now? She's
Fae. Family as much as ye."

Family.

Hugh wanted to snort, but it was true. They were
kin by marriage. "Can she...help?" He swallowed for
the hundredth time that morning.

Duncan offered another brusque nod. "She's better
than any midwife. She's wit' her now, an' my sister has
brought bairns inta tha world a 'fore. She's there as
well."

Relief made breath come easier, but only just.
Terror threatened to paralyze him. Hugh locked his
spine on Dubh's back but couldn't convince his fingers
to loosen their hold on the reins or stop shaking. "I
dinnae lose Juliette."

"*I* heard ye. *She* needs ta hear ye, MacDonald."

"Take me ta her."

I need her more than I need my next breath.

The man stared as if he could read his mind, then
turned the white horse and headed back down the road
he'd entered just moments before.

Hugh couldn't speak, so he sucked in frigid breath.
The cold seizing his lungs was cleansing in a way, but
it didn't lift his fears. His wife could still perish. The

bairn could live or die, and heir or not, he didn't want the child without Juliette.

Silence dominated as they rode past the gates, and into the inner bailey of Dunvegan castle. His voice was still gone, and all he could do was nod thanks to the lad who took Dubh toward the stables, but he was grateful that they would get his horse warm.

Hugh followed Duncan MacLeod inside, their boots the only sound echoing up the stairwell and down the long corridor. He should acknowledge the man for withholding conversation.

He looked around; nothing had changed in the year since he'd been inside the place. He'd even stayed in a guestroom when he'd brought a Fae halfling to the MacLeods for justice after she'd kidnapped Duncan's son. The lad, Lachlan, had to be three years old now, and was his nephew by marriage.

They turned a corner, and outside the very room Juliette had agreed to marry him, men were gathered. The laird, Alex, and the tall towheaded Fae man who was kin to the laird's wife. Even the old laird, Iain, was there.

"Ah, tha' was fast." Alex MacLeod pushed off the wall and extended his hand to Hugh.

"He was alreada almost here," Duncan said.

Hugh muddled his way through greetings with all the men, but his stomach was in knots. He didn't give a shite about these men or polite talk.

Juliette.

He was antsy, couldn't stand still.

"She's in there with our lasses. All is well," the Fae man said.

"'Tis right for a man ta be nervous. Ye remember well when yer lad was born, Xander, dinnae?" Iain said.

The man nodded, a smile teasing the corners of his mouth.

"Well, lad, go ta yer lass," the older man whispered. "A 'fore tha womenfolk chase us all down ta tha hall."

Four sets of eyes stared him down, as if questioning his resolve.

Hugh's heart tripped and his stomach wobbled. He whirled. Traced the outline of the closed door, as if a canyon separated him from it.

"MacDonald," Duncan said.

Hugh shot a glance over his shoulder but didn't turn around.

The MacLeod twins stood closer to each other than to Xander and Iain. They regarded him with expressions as identical as they were, but he didn't care. He needed to get to his wife.

"Remember wha' I said." Duncan lifted his chin until their eyes locked.

Hugh didn't speak. *Couldn't.*

"Tell tha' lass what she means ta ye. Before she bares yer bairn. Or Clan MacLeod will be raisin' tha MacDonald heir."

Someone snorted, but Hugh didn't retort.

He didn't have the energy to wipe the smirk off his brother-by-marriage's face, either. He wanted to murmur that Juliette knew he loved her, but if she believed that, she never would've left him, would she?

Hugh closed his eyes for a split-second. Made his feet move forward and pushed the door open.

His Juliette had asked for him.

Too bad he needed her more than she needed him. His wife was stronger than he'd ever be.

chapter seven

I t *hurt.*

More than Claire or Alana had prepped her for, and more than Jules had imagined. Hugh was a big man, and she suspected his baby was bigger than average, too. Maybe their child would rip her in half on the way out.

That's what it feels like.

The door opened as soon as another contraction hit, but her eyes locked onto her husband's, and she tried not to let the pain take over.

He's here.

Tears blurred her vision, and it wasn't because of the raging agony rolling over her middle. Jules wanted to reach for him, and she would. As soon as she could breathe again.

Duncan hadn't left that long ago—maybe a half

hour, not even enough time to get to Armadale at top speed.

How?

Did that mean he'd already been here? Had he come on his own?

Jules was too afraid to hope, so she pushed the questions away.

Hugh took one look at her and blanched. His skin was as white as the ground outside, or her bedding. His large fists were at his sides, opening and closing, and his Adam's apple bobbed — like three times. He looked like he hadn't slept in weeks, with big bags under his eyes, and the fuzz on his face was way more than a five o'clock shadow. His hair was stringy, and he looked thinner, like he'd lost a few pounds.

"Oh, Jesus," Claire muttered.

"Claire," Jules admonished.

Her sister shrugged. "What? You're the one in pain, and he looks like he's gonna friggin' pass out." She rolled her eyes.

Jules smirked. Her sister wasn't wrong.

Her man was frozen at the end of the bed, but he was still looking at her.

She couldn't look away from him.

"Sit down, before you fall over," Claire suggested. "My laird," she said, but her voice betrayed it for the afterthought it was.

Alana patted Jules' knee and pulled her nightgown back into place. "Things are progressing as they should. It shall not be long now." The princess looked at Hugh and inclined her head. "Nice to see you again, my laird."

Janet piled clean cloths next to the bed, and also greeted Hugh politely.

Her husband didn't look away from Jules as he muttered a greeting to both women.

She smiled and sniffled as a tear rolled down her cheek.

Alana tugged on Claire's hand.

Janet placed a basin of hot water on the hearth and stood, but it was all in the periphery.

Jules couldn't look away from the man she loved.

"Let's give them a moment; we have some time." The princess' voice sounded far away, but then the door shut with a soft *thud,* and the three women were gone.

"Are you gonna come over here?" she asked, but her voice was a croak. She swiped at her wet cheeks.

His face was stamped with uncertainty before he spoke. "I dinnae ken."

"You don't know?" Jules put her knuckles to the bed and pushed herself higher against the pillows at her back.

He cleared his throat and averted his gaze, but only for a second. "Are ye well?"

She smirked again, then bit her bottom lip. "Ummm, I'm having a baby. It hurts."

That seemed to jolt him into coming to her, but he

loomed above, staring. Nerves rolled off him and made her shudder.

"Hugh—"

"I dinnae bear losin' ye, Juliette."

Jules blinked.

"I dinnae bear ta lose ye, Juliette." The repetition was harder, a demand.

Her heart skipped. "Hugh," she whispered, and reached for him. His wrist was clammy beneath her fingertips, instead of the normal all-encompassing warmth.

His dark eyes found hers and the emotion there made her breathing ragged.

Jules didn't hurt at the moment, but her contractions were coming fast and intense. It wouldn't be long before she had another, and she wasn't certain her husband could handle it. She'd find it difficult to be strong for both of them.

"I dinnae bear losin' ye, Juliette," Hugh said again. This time he brought his fist up and brandished it, but his voice was thick with emotion.

She almost lost it. She sniffled and more tears were born. "You're not going to lose me."

He looked away again, like he didn't—or couldn't—believe her.

"Sit down, Hugh." She shifted closer to the middle of the big bed, her lower back twinging as she moved. She gritted her teeth. Another pain was only seconds away. Jules inhaled and closed her eyes, then blew out the air, tightening her grip on the sheet beneath her.

"Juliette?"

Finding her husband's midnight orbs helped so much, even though he'd paled again.

"Hold…hold…my hand," she begged, and he scrambled to do so, prying her fingers from the linen as the borrowed bed creaked with his added weight.

Hugh kissed her knuckles and held on, which was what she needed more than anything. "I love ye, Juliette. I love ye, *mò bhilis*." He said it over and over, and by the time the pain faded, she was crying so hard she couldn't see him.

"I love you, too," Jules whimpered.

He put his big hands on her shoulders, begging for her gaze to meet his. "I…need ta hold ye, can I hold ye?"

Jules bit her bottom lip; she was seconds from ugly-snot bawling. She nodded and buried her face against his neck. She crushed her eyes on her stupid tears, just taking him in.

Hugh smelled the same. Sandalwood and leather, mixed with winter and horse. Familiar.

Mine.

His arms were tentative around her, and she couldn't muster the energy to snuggle closer.

Their baby was demanding her attention again, and she moaned. She wanted to grab her middle. Then push.

"Juliette." Hugh's voice had a frantic edge when

he pulled back, and his eyes were wide.

"I'm okay, Hugh. Promise. Having a baby hurts."

"I dinnae lose ye." He shook his head, making his hair fly around his face. "I dinnae—"

"Hugh." Jules made his name as sharp as she could muster. "I'm not going to die. And neither is your baby."

He sat taller and swallowed again, but he didn't break their physical contact.

Jules wouldn't say his first wife's name aloud—he always winced—but she didn't believe she'd share Brenna's fate. She'd never been afraid of that, despite knowing she'd have a baby in 1676, with no pain meds or monitors. Or doctors.

Evidently *Hugh* had been worried about that for months.

Shit.

Everything clicked into place. He'd pulled away. Treated her like crap...because he was afraid, she'd die in childbirth like his first wife?

Why hadn't he just *told* her that?

"You're a huge jerk!" Jules blurted. "You almost ruined everything!"

Hugh reared back like she'd slapped him. He licked his lips but didn't say anything.

"All this time...you were afraid you'd lose me?"

Her husband flattened his mouth and nodded, but it was the barest thing, like he had trouble admitting it. Which was *totally* Hugh. Highlanders couldn't show weakness.

"You pushed me away, treated me like a leper. Made me think…" Her voice broke and she had to force a breath to speak. Had to get this out. Needed him to answer truthfully, too. "Do you want this baby, Hugh?" Tears rolled down her cheeks, but Jules avoided her husband's hands when he tried to cup her face.

He blinked and exhaled. Still didn't say a word.

Her heart stuttered. "Answer me, Hugh MacDonald."

Hugh averted the dark eyes she loved so much again. "I…" The word cracked, so he inhaled and tried again. "I was afraid ta wan' tha bairn."

Jules closed her own, and shook from the pain of an impending contraction, as well as what the man she loved had just admitted. "Hugh. Oh, Hugh."

His mouth crashed down on hers, and even though the timing was off, she kissed him back, savoring his taste. It'd been too long since he'd kissed her. Touched her, held her.

Jules needed him. Needed his strength and his love if she was going to deliver his baby safely.

The beard tickling her face was new. The hair was soft, not rough, and made her kiss him harder. Their tongues melded, danced, and fought each other for control, but pain dominated her attention and she gasped against his mouth, breaking their lip-lock.

"Oh, God." Jules rocked and rested both hands on

her seizing stomach. She could see the contraction actually rippling across her belly.

"Juliette. Juliette." Hugh had gone pallid again, despite kiss-swollen lips. "I dinnae know wha' ta do."

She blew out air, concentrating on making the agony recede. "I'll be…fine. It'll pass." She released a few more puffs and looked into her husband's eyes.

His Adam's apple jumped.

"You don't have to stay when it's time. I know that's not how it's done in this century."

"Wha' do *ye* wan' me ta do?"

Jules' heart skipped. "You'd stay with me?" she whispered. She wanted to tell him so many things, but maybe now wasn't the time.

The hurt wasn't gone entirely. He'd ruined her pregnancy, in a way. She'd been so alone. Hadn't been able to share any of the joys with him. The excitement of carrying *his* baby. First movements. Her stomach growing and the mixed emotions that'd come with that. Jitters of first-time parenthood, especially in a time when the genders weren't exactly equal.

Alana telling her the baby was a girl. Jules could tell him that, now, but if he showed disappointment that she wasn't giving him a son, it would crush her all over again.

Hugh nodded, and her breath caught when his dark eyes went misty.

"Only if you want to."

"Do ye need me, *mò bhilis*?"

A hot tear rolled down her cheek, and Jules studied him.

He thumbed it away, and the one that followed, then leaned in to press his lips to the spot.

She smiled. "I always need you, Hugh. Always."

The smile he flashed was tender and made her lose it all over again.

"I need ye, too, lass. *Tha gaol agam ort.*" The Gaelic words for *I love you* rolled off his tongue and were melt-worthy, but she needed more than that.

"I need you to need our baby, too," Jules confessed. Couldn't look at him as she awaited his answer.

Hugh's hand shook as he extended it to do something he'd never done. He caressed her distended stomach, then rested his hand against the place where their child grew. The heat of his palm seeped into her chemise.

She tried to smile through her tears, but more came. Finally, *finally,* Jules felt the connection to him and their baby at the same time.

His eyes widened as their daughter moved. "Tha…bairn?"

"She's moving around in there, but you might feel contractions, too. I think it's time. Can you get the girls? I need to push, and another pain is coming." Jules tilted her head back into the pillows and groaned. Gritted her teeth and latched onto Hugh's hand. The need to push overwhelmed.

"She?" His voice held wonder.

Jules half-snorted, half-laughed through the discomfort. "Of course, you'd focus on that." When she looked at her husband, he wore a charming smirk. "Yes, the baby's a girl. Alana told me."

His Adam's apple moved up and down. "A lass."

"Aye." Jules used his word. "Is that okay?"

The awe in his eyes made her heart miss a beat. It was genuine and endearing, and damn, she needed that, too.

"Only if she looks like ye."

She sniffled and smiled. "God, I love you. Get Alana or you're going to have to deliver your daughter."

He kissed her, hard and fast, then scrambled to his feet. A shudder wracked his frame, but at least he didn't look like a ghost this time.

chapter eight

Seeing his Juliette in so much pain petrified him as much as the fear she'd die on him. Hugh couldn't help her.

He'd never admit it aloud, but he'd not stopped to think of the child she'd carried over the course of her pregnancy. As he'd told her, he'd not thought to want *it*, because he didn't want to lose *her*. Then…touching her stomach, feeling the life inside her move against his fingertips made him swallow hard. Made his heart thump.

Hugh was going to be a father.

Today.

My bairn.

Instant love descended over him. As much for the child as for her mother.

Her.

He was to have a lassie.

If she was like his Juliette, *Jesus help me*. Hugh chuckled to himself, imagining a miniature version of his wife hollering and shaking her tiny finger at him.

Mab would be pleased, too.

"What're ye laughin' abou'? Though 'tis better than broodin'." Duncan MacLeod wore a grin again, and this time it didn't irritate him.

"My wife says 'tis time. She asks fer the lasses."

The three women, who were standing in the corridor next to their husbands, perked to attention and started chattering. They hurried past him, back into the guestroom, and he whirled to follow.

"Where're ye goin'?" Alex MacLeod asked, his voice amused.

Hugh thumbed over his shoulder. "Juliette needs me by her side."

The MacLeods exchanged looks.

Iain laughed and shook his head. "I'm goin' down ta tha hall."

"Aw, Da, ye dinnae need be in yer cups," Duncan said. He ran his hand through his long dark hair and smirked.

"Tha's what men are supposed ta do when bairns are a' comin'."

Alex laughed and shook his head. His hair swayed, but it was shorter than Duncan's, only falling right above his shoulders.

The Fae man cocked his head to one side, his

expression amused, too.

Hugh ignored them all and returned to his wife, but he had to smile. Maybe MacLeods weren't so bad after all.

His mirth was wiped away at the first look at Juliette.

Her gorgeous face was flushed red and sweat beaded her brow. Her wavy honey locks had been bound, but the look of agony on her countenance was what stilled his heart. She hurt, and he could do nothing about it.

The laird's wife was at the end of the bed, between her legs, and the dark-haired MacLeod lass was at her side. The women conversed.

His sister-by-marriage sat next to Juliette and leaned over to wipe her face with what looked to be a wet cloth.

"Hugh," Juliette breathed. "Can you come hold my hand?"

"Aye, *mò bhilis*." He hurried his step and didn't miss her sister's glare in his direction.

Hugh didn't question if Claire MacLeod didn't want him in the room or was angry at him for another reason. He just wanted to get to his Juliette.

He sat in a chair that'd been dragged to the bedside.

"My laird," his sister-by-marriage said, but her voice was too hard to consider her words a polite greeting.

"Not now, Claire," Juliette gritted out.

His wife's grip on his hand was tight, her nails digging into his skin, but it was nothing less than he deserved.

"*Now* is a perfect time." Claire turned her ire on him, full force, wearing a scowl the size of Scotland.

Hugh gave him her attention, seeing his wife in her pretty face. "Aye, my lady?" Maybe being courteous would help.

"If you hurt my sister again, I'll storm to Armadale myself to kick you in the—"

"Claire!" Juliette exclaimed. "I'm…a little…busy. Yell at him…later. I need him."

Hugh bit his tongue on the chuckle at the look Claire wore for having been cut off, lest she be offended. She'd been about to threaten his bollocks.

His sister-by-marriage stormed to the hearth, and he glanced at his wife.

His heart thumped. He leaned in and pressed a kiss to her temple. "She dinnae be wrong, *mò bhilis*. I'm sorry I hurt ye. 'Twas ne'er my intention."

"I'm not completely over it, but I will be. Thank you for being here with me." Her big green eyes were wide and misty, but some of her expression was due to physical pain.

Hugh didn't like that he could do nothing about her birthing pains, or the truth of her words, but he understood. He'd have to earn her trust again, and he'd do everything he could to help her heal, and prove he loved her — and their lassie.

He *did* want his child, and he'd wasted months. He couldn't get the time back, but he could be there for them from now on.

"Jules, with the next pain, bear down." The Fae princess patted his Juliette's bent knee and leaned in, pushing the material of her chemise higher, down her thighs, where it pooled in her lap.

The protest that she was uncovered died on his tongue. 'Twas foolish. He was the only man in the room, and the lasses needed to bare her to do their work — bring his daughter into the world.

Hugh's heart was full, and he smiled.

"Hey, don't sit there with a stupid grin on your face!" Juliette bit at him. "Help me."

He squared his shoulders and schooled his expression, fast. Did she have reason to be angry at him? He'd apologized — and meant every word.

Her sister had gone to the other side of the bed and snorted. "Don't tell me you're gonna start screaming, *'you did this to me!'* at the poor guy, Jules. You got him *in* the room. That's an accomplishment."

Juliette glared at them both.

The MacLeod lass — he thought her name was Janet — looked as if she was hiding a smile.

The laird MacLeod's wife was all seriousness as she regarded them. She looked down, as if she was checking something, then at his wife. "'Tis time, push, Jules."

Juliette nodded and a look of determination crossed her beautiful face.

She swallowed, and Hugh gripped her hand tighter, helping her the way she'd asked him to.

With every scream or moan, he winced, and still his daughter was not outside his wife's body. The more time that passed, the more panic started to encroach, but Hugh tried to suck in air and tell himself everything was fine.

The Fae princess didn't look alarmed; she kept encouraging Juliette, as were the other two lasses. Her sister kept wiping her face, and Janet breathed with her, which seemed to help lessen her pain.

His wife didn't look as if she was fading—other than appearing fatigued the longer she had to push. She braced herself on his forearm, and her sister's, her face crimson with exertion.

After another shout and a push that seemed to be ineffective, Juliette collapsed against the pillows behind her. She panted, and tears rolled down her cheeks. "I can't do it," she whimpered.

Hugh's heart skipped and his stomach clenched.

"You kinda have to," Claire said, patting her brow with the scrap of linen.

Juliette's emerald eyes locked onto him. "Hugh—"

He leaned in, cupped her face and thumbed her tears away. "Yer a strong lass. Tha strongest I've e'er met. I love ye."

The women in the room fell silent, but he didn't care. He'd help his sweet wife anyway he could, and if telling her how he felt would do it, he'd sing his love in front of every last MacLeod.

More tears were born, and he wiped them away. His gaze was still fused with his Juliette's, and one corner of her mouth lifted.

She gave a slight nod and grabbed his wrists. "Will you help me?"

Hugh nodded. "Anaway I can, *mò bhilis.*"

Seconds passed, and the lasses let him have an almost private moment with his wife, but all too soon, the princess cleared her throat.

"Let's try something," she said.

"Anathin'," he said.

"Laird MacDonald, get behind her, hold her and help her bear down. We'll get your lass out."

As they were making the necessary adjustments — Hugh moving, and Claire tossing pillows out of the way — Juliette kissed his cheek and whispered, "Thank you."

He'd never been fond of showing emotions, but his wife would reduce him to a sobbing ball if he couldn't control himself. Hugh nodded, because his voice caught in his throat. He reclined hard into the headboard behind him, and the carved wood bit into his shoulders. The jolt of discomfort was nothing compared to what she was feeling, but it grounded him, and he gently put his arms around her.

Juliette was soaked with sweat, and wet his leine, but he couldn't care less.

He was going to help her birth their child. Not many men could say they'd done the same.

She moaned as another pain came over her, and Hugh could feel it ripple over her belly under his fingertips. His wife put her head back on his shoulder and clenched her jaw. Her brows were drawn tight, and Hugh leaned forward slightly, helping her bear down, as the laird's wife had instructed. Gradually, not forcing anything that could hurt her.

"Here's her head." The princess grinned.

"Jules, you got this, push her out!" her sister said.

Juliette called his name when she started to push on her own, and he just held on, helping her use him as a lever. She gave a yell that was reminiscent of a battle cry, and then collapsed against him.

At the same time, a bairn's wail hit his ears, and Hugh's insides jumped. He wanted to look up when all three lasses made exclamations, but Juliette was staring at him, and he couldn't look away.

She closed her eyes and smiled. More tears ran down her cheeks. "Thank you, Hugh," she chanted over and over, and his chest expanded as if it would burst.

He leaned down and pressed a tender kiss to her lips. Hugh wanted more, but it wasn't the time, despite the need for more of her taste. When he'd kissed her earlier, he'd had trouble stopping. Had only done so because of her birthing pains. It'd been too long since his mouth had slanted over hers.

Serves you right.

He'd exiled himself, the wretched fool he was.

"Your lass is big and healthy!" the princess announced.

"Oh, she's so pretty, big sis!" Claire MacLeod grinned at the swaddled bundle in her arms.

The bairn had quieted but wiggled a little. Seeing the outline of the blanket move made Hugh feel better. His daughter was well, like his wife.

"I wanna see my baby," Juliette said, but her voice faded in and out, much like her expression, and her body was lax against his.

Alarm rose from his gut and latched on. "Juliette?"

Everyone paused.

The lasses had caught the panic in his voice.

His wife smiled and patted his bearded cheek. "Relax, Hugh. I'm fine. Just exhausted. Having a baby is hard. Shave this." She tugged on the hair until it smarted. "I'm glad it's soft, but it hides your beautiful face."

One of the lasses snickered, and heat rose up the back of his neck.

Hugh could do nothing but study his sweet Juliette's countenance to make sure she really was fine, and besides, it might help dispel some of his embarrassment.

She'd called him *beautiful*—with an audience.

He dared not look up at any of the MacLeod women.

Claire brought their daughter to the bedside, and one glance melted into Hugh locking eyes on the tiny form.

His breath vanished. The wee lassie had a complexion of creamy—healthy—perfection, rosebud mouth and her mother's pert little nose. Her eyes opened and closed, as if she was offended, and it made him smile. Her crown of sandy hair was visible even as she was wrapped in a soft ivory blanket, and he didn't give a damn that his vision blurred.

He'd never seen anything so gorgeous in all his two and thirty years. Hugh's hand shook as he raised it to caress her tiny head. "I'm yer da," he whispered. He was almost afraid to touch her. She looked fragile. *Helpless.* His fingers moved as if compelled. Her hair felt like silk.

Juliette squeezed his other hand and flashed a watery smile. "I want to hold her."

"As soon as Alana's done with you." Her sister smiled softly and gestured toward the end of the bed.

The princess nodded and they took care of the afterbirth, then Hugh helped her, and Janet freshen his wife up and dress her in a new chemise. He held her in his arms as they changed the bedding as well.

His sister-by-marriage had disappeared into the corridor with his daughter, and Juliette complained that she'd not even been able to hold her yet. Claire returned shortly, with her husband on her heels, and looking down into Hugh's bairn's face over his wife's shoulder.

"A wee lass," the man said.

Hugh frowned, even though there'd been no menace in the words or his tone of voice.

"What're ye goin' ta call her?" his brother-by-marriage asked.

Claire settled the infant into her mother's arms, and Juliette stared down into their daughter's face for a few moments before her eyes found Hugh's. The smile she wore was tender and made his heart flutter.

"I thought we could name her Brenna," she whispered.

He startled. His feet carried him to his wife's side of their own accord, and he had to swallow—twice. Hugh looked down at his perfect lassie, nestled against her mother's breast. "Ye…ye…would want ta do tha'?"

Juliette nodded.

His eyes blurred again, but he didn't look away from Juliette's emerald gaze. "I…" He had to clear his throat and try again. "Brenna would be honored."

She beamed and sniffled, then looked down at the bairn. "Do you want to hold her?"

Hugh's heart skipped. Of course, he did. Yet, he hesitated. She was so new…so fragile. What if he broke her?

She was a tiny thing compared to him.

He didn't know how to hold a wee bairn.

"I do." Duncan swept to the bed and Juliette smiled as she handed the child over. "'Tis only a wee lassie, nothin' ta fear, a'tall." Hugh's brother-by-marriage handled his bairn as if he was a nursemaid, and not Alex MacLeod's war chief. He looked *comfortable*. "Ye jus' have ta make sure ya support her head." He held the tiny lass against his chest, too close to MacLeod plaid for Hugh's comfort.

The man flashed a grin he wanted to wipe off his face. It was one Juliette would've called, *smart arsed.*

"Give me my lassie!" he growled.

Duncan ignored him, staring down into the little face Hugh wanted to get another look at, too. He let out a low whistle. "I'm relieved."

"Abou' what?" Hugh demanded.

His rival flashed another grin. "Tha lassie resembles her mother."

He snarled, but the women within hearing—and the laird, who stood at the doorway—laughed.

"Give. Me. My. Lassie."

Unrepentant, Duncan beamed, but the man came to his side and gently transferred his daughter to his arms.

Hugh didn't move. Had to remind himself to breathe. Definitely ignored the obvious amusement going around the room. He only had eyes for the bairn in his hands.

She weighed more than she appeared to, was a solid warmth against his chest. That made him feel better about holding her. Her face was angelic, and she'd fallen asleep, which made her seem even more perfect.

"Brenna," he breathed. His gaze found his wife's, and she was crying again.

He crossed the room to her and sat gently on the edge of the bed beside her, doing his best not to disturb his sleeping daughter, or cause any lingering discomfort to his Juliette.

As he understood it, new bairns didn't sleep much, so he could only hope his wee lass would remain so as long as possible, so his wife could also rest. They both needed to recover from the birth. Hell, he needed to recover from it, too.

His wife was a warrior. Juliette was tougher than any man he knew, including himself. Were it up to men, there wouldn't be bairns.

Hugh was barely aware that all the MacLeods had cleared out, leaving him alone with his lasses.

♡ ♡ ♡

Jules watched her big strong Highlander practically melt when he took their daughter from her brother-in-law. Which in turn, melted *her*, making her cry for the millionth time. She'd become a huge, sappy baby.

She regretted that they didn't have cameras. The look on Hugh's face was incomparable. Beautiful, despite the face-fur that needed to go. She'd remember that look for the rest of her life.

"Juliette," he practically purred her name. "Why're ye cryin', *mò bhilis*?" Hugh caressed her face with shaky fingers, his huge palm holding the baby's head to his chest.

"Seeing you with her. The way you're looking at her. It's all I ever wanted, Hugh." Jules had to sniffle through her words, but she sucked in a breath and tried to get a hold of herself. "I was so afraid—"

"Nay, love. Dinnae say it. 'Tis over, an' forgive me fer bein' an arse. I'm here. Dinnae be goin' anawhere."

"Good." She smiled.

Hugh looked down into their daughter's perfect little face and his expression was about as tender as she'd ever seen. Love and devotion written all over it.

Jules had fallen in love with their child before Brenna had even moved within her for the first time, but to see him fall for her too, made her insides wobble.

Finally.

Their happily ever after could resume.

Her life—her heart—was full.

"I do forgive you," she whispered.

His dark eyes locked onto hers and he smiled—slowly. It was sexy, even with the beard.

How she could think so after just having a baby was a wonder, but Hugh certainly hadn't lost his appeal—thank God.

She wanted to kiss him. Later. Maybe after a nap.

Her husband handed her the baby and Jules

grinned as Brenna fussed when she woke in the transfer. The look of panic on his face was priceless.

"Relax, Hugh, she's probably hungry. She's gonna do this crying thing a lot, you know. You'll have to get used to it."

Hugh nodded, but his gaze was on the breast she was baring.

"If I can't do this right, I might need Alana to—" but Brenna latched on like a pro and started to suckle. Jules tried not to wince at the prickles that shot through her nipple. It didn't hurt with any severity, but it didn't feel awesome, either.

Fascination was all over her husband's face.

"Oh geesh," she whispered, which made his eyes meet hers.

"'Tis beautiful."

Heat kissed her neck and cheeks, and she looked down at the baby. She was going to chide him for being all about her boobs, but he wasn't. He was awed by her feeding their child and that was just—*wow*, in a good way.

He was gorgeous. He was hers again, and *she* was kinda in awe of that.

Hugh caressed their baby's downy hair as she nursed. "I dinnae ken if I can do this again."

He sounded so serious, Jules didn't want to give into the laugh, but she couldn't help it.

"You? What about me? I'm the one who had to carry her all these months, get *huge*, then hurt worse than I ever have." She smiled at her daughter. "Although, she was worth it." When she looked at her husband, his beautiful dark eyes had gone misty again—and her heart stuttered.

"Juliette—"

She reached for his hand and squeezed. "I know."

His Adam's apple dipped, but he nodded, too.

Jules had gotten a Valentine's Day present after all. The best one. *Ever*.

"I love you. I love her, too. More than words. Happy Valentine's Day, Hugh."

"I love ye, both. My lasses." His expression was impossibly soft. Loving, as he regarded his tiny daughter. Hugh met her eyes again, his brows knitted. "But, *mò bhilis*, what's…Valentine's Day…did ye say? Do ye mean Saint Valentine?"

She just grinned.

epilogue

hugh dropped an article of clothing with every step as he crossed the room. He wasn't walking. Her husband was prowling.

The intensity in his dark eyes named Jules his prey, but she would've begged for it anyway. That look made her combust from the inside out. Every nerve ending seared for him, and he hadn't laid a finger on her…yet.

He stopped in front of her naked. His erection—always impressive, anyway—jutted toward her as if beckoning on its own.

Damn…she needed to touch him. Taste him.

Jules shivered.

"Undress," Hugh growled.

He didn't have to tell her twice.

Her mouth was too dry for words, so she forced a nod and watched his muscles ripple with obvious impatience. Her man quivered, his desire a live thing Jules fed off. Her sex throbbed in response.

Shaky hands grabbed the sides of her sleeping chemise as if they weren't her own.

"Ye take too long." Hugh reached for her, tugging the material up and helping her get her arms free before one last yank over her head.

Then he swept her off her feet, before the soft fabric even hit the stone floor or the chill in the room could seep into her bare skin.

Jules yelped; he'd caught her off guard, but she shouldn't have been surprised. Rough and raw was how she loved this man, and it'd been too long since he'd had his hands on her.

His lips crashed down on hers, but she didn't hesitate to twine her tongue around his. Hugh dominated her mouth like he owned her heart and kissed her until her need of him shot all over her body like little arrows.

First brush of his fingers between her legs and she'd come, she burned for him so badly.

Hugh tossed her onto the bed and the breath left her lungs, but Jules didn't give a damn.

She opened her arms, ready to have him on top of her, inside her.

Now.

Instead of coming to her, her husband stood beside the bed and stared down. Licked his kiss-swollen lips, too, which made her stomach wobble.

Jules squirmed, wanting to cover her still-not-flat tummy, and hide her stretch marks. Their daughter was two months old now; her body still wasn't the same, despite the runs she'd started doing on the frigid beach—regardless of Hugh's protests. It was April, but spring was being a tease, and it was still freezing most mornings.

He'd started running with her, if only to keep her from being unguarded, so they'd made it a competition. He was damn hard to keep up with since he was so much taller, but she'd beat him this morning.

She'd sealed her win with an overheated kiss, but Hugh had backed off. Disappointingly so. She would've stripped for him right then and there—temperature be damned.

Jules had been begging him to make love to her for weeks.

Hugh had been worried she wasn't healed—despite the fact she'd assured him Alana had helped with that—with magic. She'd healed faster than she normally would have on her own. Been ready to go for a whole month.

Tonight, she'd dared him with one too many kisses after dinner. Jules had won. She'd have him. Right now.

Damn good thing he was finally on the same page with her.

Hugh groaned. "*Mò bhilis*, yer so bonnie."

She swallowed and pushed to her knees, meeting him at the edge of the bed. She didn't want to talk about her body's imperfections. If she denied his words, he'd just argue—or assert—that he was right. She wanted her man in her arms.

Jules dragged two fingers down his pecs, following the curve of his dark areolas, and petting his nipples until they pushed back, hard flat little tips. She stroked the tight curls that dotted the expanse, then went downward, tracing his defined abs, parting his happy trail, and teasing the tip of his bobbing cock with her palm.

With every noise he emitted, she bloomed even more for him. Need was eating her up. Her thighs shook and her clit pulsed. Jules could feel a new rush of moisture from her core.

Hugh pushed at her shoulders, encouraging her to lie back as he placed a knee between her legs. The move was rather gentle for her normally demanding barbarian.

"Hugh?" she whispered.

"I need ye, *mò bhilis.*" His grip on her upper arms was loose, despite the tension in his words.

"I need you, too. Thought that's what this is about. Have me, Hugh. Take me."

His dark eyes flashed, and her husband didn't hesitate to cover her body with his. He still wasn't as rough as usual, especially given how high his blood must be singing. It'd been a *long* time since they'd had sex.

Jules closed her eyes and kissed his shoulder. She

slid her arms around him, loving the press of his hips against hers. His hard stomach over her softer one. His chest against her breasts, even though they were sore from nursing Brenna.

Hugh's heat washed over her and made her heart beat even faster than the mutual arousal already had it. The rough springy hair on his legs only amped her higher. Every inch of him was against every inch of her, and it was about damn time.

"I love you," Jules panted.

He pulled back and looked down at her before pressing a gentle kiss to her lips. "I love ye, my sweet wife. My Juliette."

She kissed him again, but it wasn't soft. She urged him with her tongue, thrusting it in and out of his mouth, squeezing her arms around his neck.

His erection burned her inner thigh, but he wasn't in the right place.

Jules slid her hand between them and gripped him.

Hugh gasped into their kiss. "Juliette…"

"Get inside me, Hugh MacDonald."

"I dinnae want ta hurt ye wit' my eagerness."

"*I* am more eager than you."

"Aye?" Challenge glinted in his gorgeous midnight eyes, and he smirked.

She traced his lips with her fingertip, outlining that sexy expression. "Do ya wanna bet me? That didn't work so well for you this morning on the beach."

Hugh growled and caught her finger in his teeth, but he didn't hurt her. He sucked, teasing her skin with his tongue.

Jules moaned and desire unfurled in her belly all over again, lower. Hotter.

Without breaking their eye contact, Hugh shifted his pelvis away only to come back, filling her with one hard stroke that took her breath and flooded her with pleasure.

Instead of starting to thrust, like she *needed*, her husband stilled, hovering.

"Did I hurt ye?" It was a strained demand that snapped her back into her skin.

"No. God, no. Move, please move, Hugh. I need you. *All* of you." Jules slid her legs around his waist to assist her plea and squeezed her thighs.

He grunted and moved his hips away only to drive forward again—finally.

She sensed some remaining hesitation, but when Jules slammed her mouth into his, Hugh got with the program. He kissed her deeper; took her hard and fast, exactly what she wanted.

His tongue worked in time with his thrusts, making them soar higher and higher. He never stopped kissing her, sampling her mouth as if he couldn't get enough of her taste.

The feeling was mutual.

Jules dragged her hands over his sweaty shoulders and down his back, kneading his perfect ass and urging him even faster.

Ecstasy made her muscles tremble, and she shook in his arms as orgasm crashed over her. It was intense, and sucked away her air, but she didn't care, because pleasure made her head spin as her inner muscles contracted and relaxed.

Hugh wasn't far behind. His biceps went taut first, before his spine stiffened, and he broke their kiss, burying his face against the damp skin of her neck. He breathed her name like a chant as his release shot deep and the aftershock of her climax milked him.

They panted against each other, his massive chest heaving, forcing his chest hair to tickle her overheated skin. Jules quaked, but she wasn't cold.

Silence descended, but it was okay, because she couldn't speak just yet.

Being with her husband again was better than she'd remembered—imagined. Better than before. He'd rocked her world again.

Made her feel him *completely*. Connected. Loved. Worshiped.

Jules tightened her grip around him. She couldn't see his face, but she planted a kiss next to his ear and smiled when he shuddered against her. His stubble brushed her skin. "*Tha gaol agam ort,*" she whispered.

Hugh lifted his head, and the sexy smirk was back in place. "That dinnae be half bad, lass. And I love ye, too." He went to move off her, but she held him fast, and her man chuckled.

"Wait. Please don't go. I need to feel you."

Concern crossed his handsome face. "I'll no' leave ye, *mò bhilis,* I jus' dinnae want ta crush ye."

"You're not hurting me."

Hugh dipped down and took her mouth, kissing Jules until her already boneless form melted even more.

She loosened her hold, and her husband slipped from her body and nestled next to her on his side.

"See? I'm here wit' ye."

Jules snuggled into him, and he caressed her back in the long soothing strokes she'd always loved. "Always."

"Always," he repeated, and gave a curt nod.

She cocked her head to one side, her hair shifting to tickle her shoulder. "Well, at least for a few more hours, until your daughter wails and you pretend you're sleeping through it." He opened his mouth, but Jules cut him off with a mock-glare. "Don't you dare deny it." She poked his chest.

Hugh batted her hand away, but then caught it and kissed her knuckles. "Love, I dinnae—"

When she arched an eyebrow at him, he chuckled.

"Och!" She stole one of Mab's favorite words. "I knew it!"

He surged forward and covered her mouth with his, slipping his hand to the back of her neck, tangling his fingers in her natural waves, and pulling her closer.

Fortunately for him, he was a good enough kisser that she embraced the distraction but wasn't dumb enough not to spot it for what it was from a mile away.

Jules would get him back, but it would have to be… later.

Her husband nudged her legs open and stroked two fingers up and down her sex, then paid close attention to her already throbbing clit.

She tilted her head back and moaned.

Later…indeed.

the end

note to the Reader:

Jules and Hugh were two of those characters who just didn't feel "done" when I was finished with their book, *The Parchment Scroll (Highland Secrets Trilogy Book Three),* so this story was born, but I knew the subject matter was something they would have to deal with from the start. It'd been floating around in my head since I typed "The End" the first time around.

I love Hugh, just LOVE him (don't tell my other heroes…LOL) so I loved getting back in his head for *Highland Valentine.*

If you haven't read their love story, you can keep reading here and check out the first chapter of *The Parchment Scroll.* It's the third book in my trilogy, but you can read the books out of order, they are all standalone within the series. I have details on my "Other Books by C.A. Szarek" page for the order of the series, as well as all the other books that are associated.

about the author

USA Today Bestselling, award winning author of romantic suspense, epic and historical fantasy romance, C.A. loves to dabble in different genres. If it's a good story, she'll write it, no matter where it seems to fit!

She's a hopeless romantic and always will be. Risking it all for Happily Ever After is what she lives by!

C.A. is originally from Ohio, but got to Texas as soon as she could. She's happily married and has a bachelor's degree in Criminal Justice.

She's always writing, and helps small business owners by writing their websites, and she loves it!

WEBSITE: http://www.caszarek.com
EBOOK STORE:

https://www.caszarek.com/ebook-store
PAPERBACK STORE:
https://www.caszarek.com/paperback-store
FACEBOOK:
http://www.facebook.com/caszarek
INSTAGRAM:
https://www.instagram.com/caszarek/
TWITTER: https://twitter.com/caszarek
BOOKBUB:
https://www.bookbub.com/profile/c-a-szarek
GOODREADS:
https://www.goodreads.com/author/show/5815085.
C_A_Szarek
EMAIL: ca@caszarek.com

You can sign up for C.A.'s newsletter on her website, as well as buy all her books!